The Twelve Tribes

Christian fiction, Volume 7

Gregory Allen Parker

Published by Graywolf Press, 2024.

THE TWELVE TRIBES

First edition. August 8, 2024.

Copyright © 2024 Gregory Allen Parker.

ISBN: 979-8227362339

Written by Gregory Allen Parker.

Table of Contents

To those who seek the wisdom of the ancients and the faith to
navigate the present,

To the steadfast souls who find strength in the promises of old and the
hope in the promises yet to come,

And to my family, whose unwavering support and love make every
journey possible.

May this work inspire, guide, and remind us all of the enduring legacy
of the Twelve Tribes of Israel and the timeless truths they represent.

Chapter 1: The Promise

Summary: The chapter introduces the origins of the Twelve Tribes of Israel, beginning with God's promise to Abraham.

Bible Verse: Genesis 12:2-3 - "I will make you into a great nation, and I will bless you; I will make your name great, and you will be a blessing. I will bless those who bless you, and whoever curses you I will curse; and all peoples on earth will be blessed through you."

Chapter 1: The Promise

In the beginning, before the tribes of Israel took form, before the sands of time could trace their lineage, there was a man chosen by God to be the father of many nations. This man, Abram, lived in a time where polytheism was rampant, and the idea of one true God was foreign to the people around him. Yet, it was to Abram that the one true God, Yahweh, spoke, initiating a promise that would reverberate through the generations and shape the destiny of a people chosen for His purposes.

Abram was born in the city of Ur of the Chaldeans, a bustling metropolis of its time, known for its ziggurats and a pantheon of gods. Despite the thriving culture and economic prosperity of Ur, Abram's heart yearned for something more, a divine purpose that was yet to be revealed to him. It was in this setting that Yahweh's voice broke through the clamor of false gods, calling Abram to a higher calling.

"Leave your country, your people and your father's household and go to the land I will show you," said the Lord. These were not merely words of direction but a divine mandate that required Abram to abandon all that he knew. The call of God was clear and uncompromising, demanding a faith that would be the cornerstone of the covenant that Yahweh was establishing.

Abram, in obedience to the call, departed from Ur, accompanied by his wife Sarai, his nephew Lot, and all their possessions and servants. Their journey took them to Haran, a place of temporary settlement. Even in Haran, the voice of the Lord persisted, reminding Abram of the promise and the necessity of his continued faithfulness.

The promise made to Abram was profound and expansive. God said, "I will make you into a great nation, and I will bless you; I will make your name great, and you will be a blessing. I will bless those who bless you, and whoever curses you I will curse; and all peoples on earth will be blessed through you" (Genesis 12:2-3). This promise encapsulated not only the future of Abram's descendants but also the divine intention to bless all the nations of the earth through his lineage.

With renewed determination, Abram left Haran, journeying towards Canaan, the land that God had promised to show him. This journey was not without challenges. The land of Canaan was already inhabited by various tribes, and Abram's entourage had to navigate through these territories. Nevertheless, Abram's faith remained steadfast, and he built altars to Yahweh along the way, marking the places where God had spoken to him.

Upon arriving in Canaan, God appeared to Abram and reiterated the promise: "To your offspring I will give this land." This reaffirmation was a testament to God's unwavering commitment to His covenant. Abram's response was to build another altar, dedicating the land and his journey to the God who had called him.

However, the fulfillment of God's promise did not come immediately. Abram and Sarai faced the reality of their old age and the barrenness that had plagued them. Despite their doubts and moments of human frailty, God's promise stood firm. In a profound act of faith, Abram believed God, and it was credited to him as righteousness.

The story of Abram, who would later be known as Abraham, is a tapestry of faith, obedience, and divine assurance. As years passed, the promise of a son seemed increasingly improbable, yet God's timing and purpose were perfect. At the appointed time, the Lord appeared to Abraham and declared that Sarai, now Sarah, would bear a son. This son, Isaac, was the child of promise, through whom the covenant would be established and carried forward.

Isaac's birth was a miraculous event, a testament to God's faithfulness. Abraham's joy was boundless, and he named his son Isaac, meaning "he laughs," reflecting the joy and disbelief that Sarah had expressed at the news of her pregnancy. Isaac's birth was not merely a fulfillment of a personal promise to Abraham and Sarah but a pivotal moment in the divine plan for humanity.

As Isaac grew, he became the bearer of the promise. The same covenant that God had made with Abraham was reaffirmed to Isaac, establishing a continuity that would extend through the generations. Isaac married Rebekah, and they had two sons, Esau and Jacob. While Esau was the elder, it was Jacob who was chosen by God to carry forward the covenant.

Jacob's story is one of transformation and divine encounter. Known initially for his cunning and deceit, Jacob's life took a pivotal turn when he wrestled with an angel of the Lord at Peniel. This encounter left him with a limp but also a new name, Israel, meaning "he struggles with God." It was through Jacob, now Israel, that the promise to Abraham continued to unfold.

Israel had twelve sons, each of whom became the progenitor of the Twelve Tribes of Israel. These sons were Reuben, Simeon, Levi, Judah, Dan, Naphtali, Gad, Asher, Issachar, Zebulun, Joseph, and Benjamin. Each son carried a part of the promise, and their descendants would form the nation of Israel, a people chosen by God to be a light to the nations.

The story of the Twelve Tribes begins with a promise, a divine declaration that set into motion the events that would shape the history of a people and, ultimately, the world. This promise was not just for Abraham and his immediate descendants but was a foreshadowing of the ultimate blessing that would come through the lineage of Abraham - the Messiah, Jesus Christ, through whom all nations would indeed be blessed.

In understanding the origins of the Twelve Tribes, one must grasp the significance of God's promise to Abraham. It was a promise that required faith, obedience, and perseverance. It was a promise that transcended human limitations and doubts. It was a promise that demonstrated God's sovereign plan and His unwavering faithfulness.

The journey of Abraham from Ur to Canaan, the birth of Isaac, the transformation of Jacob to Israel, and the establishment of the Twelve Tribes are all integral parts of the fulfillment of God's promise. This promise is a testament to God's enduring commitment to His people and His plan of redemption for all humanity.

As we delve deeper into the stories of the Twelve Tribes, we will see how this divine promise unfolds through the lives of the patriarchs, the challenges they faced, and the victories they achieved. The promise to Abraham is the foundation upon which the history of the Israelites is built, and it serves as a reminder of God's unchanging faithfulness and His desire to bless all the nations of the earth.

The legacy of the Twelve Tribes is not merely a historical account but a living testimony of God's promise and purpose. It is a story that continues to inspire faith and obedience, calling us to trust in the promises of God and to walk in the footsteps of those who have gone before us. Through the Twelve Tribes, we see the unfolding of a divine narrative that points us to the ultimate fulfillment of God's promise in Jesus Christ, the Savior of the world.

In the early years of Abram's journey, the path was fraught with uncertainty and challenge. The land of Canaan, although promised, was not readily accessible. It was a land inhabited by formidable tribes and peoples, each with their own customs and gods. Yet, Abram's faith did not waver. He journeyed through the land, building altars to Yahweh, marking each place where God reaffirmed His promise.

One such place was Shechem, where the Lord appeared to Abram and said, "To your offspring I will give this land" (Genesis 12:7). This promise was not only a personal assurance to Abram but also a declaration of God's sovereignty over the land and its inhabitants. In response, Abram built an altar to the Lord, establishing a place of worship and remembrance.

From Shechem, Abram moved to the hills east of Bethel and pitched his tent, with Bethel on the west and Ai on the east. Here again, he built an altar to the Lord and called on the name of Yahweh. Abram's journey was marked by these acts of worship, signifying his dependence on and devotion to the God who had called him.

Despite his faithfulness, Abram faced trials that tested his trust in God's promise. A severe famine struck the land of Canaan, forcing Abram to go down to Egypt to survive. This detour was a test of faith, as Abram had to navigate the complexities of a foreign land while maintaining his integrity. In Egypt, Abram's fear for his safety led him to misrepresent his relationship with Sarai, telling the Egyptians that she was his sister. This deception brought about complications, but God's protection was evident as He intervened to ensure Abram's safety and integrity.

Upon returning to Canaan, Abram and Lot, his nephew, faced another challenge. Their combined wealth and herds had grown so large that the land could not support them both. To prevent conflict, Abram generously offered

Lot the first choice of land. Lot chose the fertile plains of the Jordan Valley, while Abram remained in the land of Canaan. This act of selflessness was a testament to Abram's faith in God's provision and promise.

After Lot's departure, God once again spoke to Abram, reaffirming the promise: "Lift up your eyes from where you are and look north and south, east and west. All the land that you see I will give to you and your offspring forever" (Genesis 13:14-15). This reiteration of the promise was a reassurance of God's unwavering commitment to His covenant with Abram.

As time passed, Abram continued to walk in faith, building altars and worshiping Yahweh. His journey was marked by divine encounters that reinforced the promise and guided his steps. One significant encounter occurred at Hebron, where Abram settled by the great trees of Mamre and built an altar to the Lord.

In the midst of these journeys and divine encounters, Abram's relationship with God deepened. He was known as a friend of God, a title that reflected his close communion with the Creator. This relationship was pivotal in the unfolding of God's plan, as Abram's faith and obedience became the foundation upon which the covenant was built.

The promise to Abram was not limited to land and descendants but extended to the blessing of all nations. This aspect of the promise was a foreshadowing of the redemptive plan that would culminate in the coming of Jesus Christ, the Messiah. Through Abram's lineage, the Savior of the world would come, bringing salvation and blessing to all who believe.

The journey of faith that began with Abram continued through his son Isaac. Isaac, the child of promise, was born to Abram and Sarai in their old age, a miraculous fulfillment of God's word. The birth of Isaac was a pivotal moment, as it marked the continuation of the covenant and the realization of God's promise.

Isaac's life was marked by his own encounters with God, who reaffirmed the covenant made with Abram. Like his father, Isaac faced challenges and tests of faith, yet God's faithfulness remained steadfast. Isaac married Rebekah, and they had two sons, Esau and Jacob. While Esau was the elder, it was Jacob who was chosen by God to carry forward the covenant.

Jacob's story is one of transformation and divine encounter. Known initially for his cunning and deceit, Jacob's life took a pivotal turn when he wrestled with an angel of the Lord at Peniel. This encounter left him with a limp but also a new name, Israel, meaning "he struggles with God." It was through Jacob, now Israel, that the promise to Abraham continued to unfold.

Israel had twelve sons, each of whom became the progenitor of the Twelve Tribes of Israel. These sons were Reuben, Simeon, Levi, Judah, Dan, Naphtali, Gad, Asher, Issachar, Zebulun, Joseph, and Benjamin. Each son carried a part of the promise, and their descendants would form the nation of Israel, a people chosen by God to be a light to the nations.

The story of the Twelve Tribes begins with a promise, a divine declaration that set into motion the events that would shape the history of a people and, ultimately, the world. This promise was not just for Abraham and his immediate descendants but was a foreshadowing of the ultimate blessing that would come through the lineage of Abraham - the Messiah, Jesus Christ, through whom all nations would indeed be blessed.

In understanding the origins of the Twelve Tribes, one must grasp the significance of God's promise to Abraham. It was a promise that required faith, obedience, and perseverance. It was a promise that transcended human limitations and doubts. It was a promise that demonstrated God's sovereign plan and His unwavering faithfulness.

The journey of Abraham from Ur to Canaan, the birth of Isaac, the transformation of Jacob to Israel, and the establishment of the Twelve Tribes are all integral parts of the fulfillment of God's promise. This promise is a testament to God's enduring commitment to His people and His plan of redemption for all humanity.

As we delve deeper into the stories of the Twelve Tribes, we will see how this divine promise unfolds through the lives of the patriarchs, the challenges they faced, and the victories they achieved. The promise to Abraham is the foundation upon which the history of the Israelites is built, and it serves as a reminder of God's unchanging faithfulness and His desire to bless all the nations of the earth.

The legacy of the Twelve Tribes is not merely a historical account but a living testimony of God's promise and purpose. It is a story that continues to inspire faith and obedience, calling us to trust in the promises of God and to walk in the footsteps of those who have gone before us. Through the Twelve

Tribes, we see the unfolding of a divine narrative that points us to the ultimate fulfillment of God's promise in Jesus Christ, the Savior of the world.

As the narrative continues, the focus shifts to the development of the covenant through Abraham's lineage. The birth of Isaac was a significant event, not just for Abraham and Sarah, but for the future of the covenant. Isaac represented the tangible fulfillment of God's promise, a beacon of hope that God's word was steadfast and true.

Isaac's own journey of faith began under the shadow of his father's legacy. He inherited not only the wealth and status of Abraham but also the divine promise. Isaac's life, though less tumultuous than his father's, was not without its trials. Famine once again struck the land, and Isaac found himself contemplating a move to Egypt, just as his father had done. However, God appeared to Isaac and commanded him to stay in the land of Gerar, promising to bless him and confirm the oath He had sworn to Abraham.

Isaac obeyed, and God blessed him abundantly. His crops flourished, his herds multiplied, and his wealth increased, provoking jealousy among the Philistines. Despite the hostility, Isaac remained steadfast, digging wells to sustain his household and herds. Each time the Philistines contested his wells, Isaac moved on and dug another, demonstrating patience and reliance on God's provision.

In a reaffirmation of the covenant, God appeared to Isaac at Beersheba, saying, "I am the God of your father Abraham. Do not be afraid, for I am with you; I will bless you and will increase the number of your descendants for the sake of my servant Abraham" (Genesis 26:24). Isaac built an altar there and called on the name of the Lord, solidifying his commitment to the covenant and his trust in God's promises.

Isaac's marriage to Rebekah brought forth twins, Esau and Jacob. From their birth, it was evident that the two sons represented divergent paths. Esau, the elder, was a skilled hunter, favored by Isaac, while Jacob was a quiet man, dwelling in tents, favored by Rebekah. The prophecy given to Rebekah during her pregnancy, "Two nations are in your womb, and two peoples from within you will be separated; one people will be stronger than the other, and the older will serve the younger" (Genesis 25:23), hinted at the significant roles they would play in the unfolding of God's plan.

Jacob, despite his initial deceptive ways, was the chosen vessel through whom the promise would continue. His journey from deceit to transformation was marked by divine encounters and struggles that shaped his character and destiny. The turning point in Jacob's life came at Bethel, where he dreamt of a ladder reaching to heaven, with angels ascending and descending on it. In the dream, God stood above the ladder and reiterated the promise made to Abraham and Isaac: "I am the LORD, the God of your father Abraham and the God of Isaac. I will give you and your descendants the land on which you are lying. Your descendants will be like the dust of the earth" (Genesis 28:13-14).

Awed by the vision, Jacob made a vow, declaring Bethel a holy place and promising to serve God faithfully. This encounter marked the beginning of Jacob's transformation and his journey towards becoming Israel, the father of the Twelve Tribes.

Jacob's life was a tapestry of struggles, both physical and spiritual. His journey to Paddan Aram to seek a wife led him to his uncle Laban, where he experienced years of labor and deception. Despite the challenges, Jacob's faith grew, and he prospered, marrying Leah and Rachel and fathering twelve sons and a daughter. Each son, born through both Leah, Rachel, and their maidservants Bilhah and Zilpah, represented the future tribes of Israel.

The culmination of Jacob's transformation came when he wrestled with a divine being at Peniel. This encounter, intense and transformative, left Jacob physically altered with a limp but spiritually renewed with a new name, Israel. The name signified his struggle with God and men and his prevailing faith. This moment was pivotal, solidifying Jacob's role as the patriarch through whom the covenant would be carried forward.

The narrative of the Twelve Tribes gains depth as we delve into the lives of Jacob's sons, each of whom played a critical role in the formation of the nation of Israel. Reuben, the firstborn, faced his own trials and redemption. Simeon and Levi, known for their fierce loyalty and sometimes rash actions, had their own paths of growth. Judah emerged as a leader among his brothers, and his lineage would ultimately lead to the birth of King David and, eventually, Jesus Christ.

Joseph, one of the most prominent figures among Jacob's sons, experienced a journey from suffering to triumph that mirrored the larger narrative of the Israelites. Sold into slavery by his jealous brothers, Joseph rose to prominence in Egypt, becoming a powerful figure who ultimately saved his family from famine. His story is a testament to God's providence and the fulfillment of the promise, as he declared to his brothers, "You intended to harm me, but God intended it for good to accomplish what is now being done, the saving of many lives" (Genesis 50:20).

The Twelve Tribes of Israel, born from the twelve sons of Jacob, each carried a unique identity and destiny. As they grew into a nation, their stories intertwined with the divine promise given to Abraham.

The land of Canaan, promised to Abraham, Isaac, and Jacob, became the stage upon which their faith and struggles played out.

The establishment of the tribes was not without its challenges. The journey from Egypt, through the wilderness, and into the Promised Land was marked by trials and triumphs. The leadership of Moses and Joshua was crucial in guiding the tribes, ensuring that the promise of God remained central to their identity and purpose.

The division of the land among the tribes, as described in the book of Joshua, was a fulfillment of the promise and a testament to God's faithfulness. Each tribe received its inheritance, a tangible representation of the covenant. Yet, the possession of the land required continued faith and obedience. The era of the Judges highlighted the cyclical pattern of faithfulness and rebellion, underscoring the need for steadfastness in following God's commands.

The promise to Abraham, reaffirmed to Isaac and Jacob, was a thread that wove through the history of the Israelites. It was a promise of land, descendants, and blessing that found its ultimate fulfillment in Jesus Christ. Through the lineage of Abraham, Isaac, and Jacob, the Messiah came, bringing salvation and blessing to all nations.

The story of the Twelve Tribes is a testament to God's unwavering faithfulness and His desire to bless humanity. It is a story that calls us to faith, obedience, and perseverance. As we journey through the lives of the patriarchs and the tribes, we are reminded of the divine promise that transcends time and circumstance. It is a promise that invites us to trust in God's plan and to walk in the legacy of faith left by those who have gone before us.

The legacy of the Twelve Tribes is not merely a historical account but a living testimony of God's promise and purpose. It is a story that continues to inspire faith and obedience, calling us to trust in the promises of God and to walk in the footsteps of those who have gone before us. Through the Twelve Tribes, we see the unfolding of a divine narrative that points us to the ultimate fulfillment of God's promise in Jesus Christ, the Savior of the world.

In the beginning, there was a promise. A promise that set into motion a journey of faith, obedience, and divine purpose. A promise that transcended human limitations and doubts. A promise that demonstrated God's sovereign plan and His unwavering faithfulness. This promise, given to Abraham, carried through Isaac and Jacob, and embodied in the Twelve Tribes, is a testament to God's enduring commitment to His people and His plan of redemption for all humanity.

The promise to Abraham is the foundation upon which the history of the Israelites is built, and it serves as a reminder of God's unchanging faithfulness and His desire to bless all the nations of the earth. It is a story that continues to inspire faith and obedience, calling us to trust in the promises of God and to walk in the footsteps of those who have gone before us. Through the Twelve Tribes, we see the unfolding of a divine narrative that points us to the ultimate fulfillment of God's promise in Jesus Christ, the Savior of the world.

In the final section of this chapter, we reflect on the enduring significance of the promise to Abraham. The narrative of the Twelve Tribes is not just a historical recounting but a profound theological reflection on God's faithfulness and the unfolding of His redemptive plan.

Abraham's journey from Ur to Canaan was a journey of faith that required him to leave behind everything familiar and to trust in God's promise. This journey was marked by altars and acts of worship, signifying Abraham's dependence on and devotion to Yahweh. Each altar was a testament to God's faithfulness and a marker of the journey toward the fulfillment of the promise.

The birth of Isaac was a miraculous event that demonstrated God's power and faithfulness. Despite their old age, Abraham and Sarah experienced the fulfillment of God's promise in the birth of their son. Isaac's life, marked by his own encounters with God, continued the narrative of the covenant. His marriage to Rebekah and the birth of Esau and Jacob furthered the unfolding of God's plan.

Jacob's transformation into Israel, marked by his divine encounter at Peniel, was a pivotal moment in the narrative. His twelve sons, each carrying a part of the promise, became the progenitors of the Twelve Tribes of Israel. Their lives and journeys intertwined with the divine promise, shaping the destiny of the nation of Israel.

The narrative of the Twelve Tribes is a testament to God's faithfulness and His desire to bless all nations. Through the lineage of Abraham, Isaac, and Jacob, the Messiah came, bringing salvation and blessing to all who believe. This promise, fulfilled in Jesus Christ, is the ultimate expression of God's love and faithfulness.

As we conclude this chapter, we are reminded of the enduring significance of the promise to Abraham. It is a promise that calls us to faith, obedience, and perseverance. It is a promise that transcends time and circumstance, inviting us to trust in God's plan and to walk in the legacy of faith left by those who have gone before us. Through the Twelve Tribes, we see the unfolding of a divine narrative that points us to the ultimate fulfillment of God's promise in Jesus Christ, the Savior of the world.

Bible Verse: Genesis 12:2-3 - "I will make you into a great nation, and I will bless you; I will make your name great, and you will be a blessing. I will bless those who bless you, and whoever curses you I will curse; and all peoples on earth will be blessed through you."

This promise, given to Abraham, is the foundation of the narrative of the Twelve Tribes. It is a promise that demonstrates God's sovereign plan and His unwavering faithfulness. As we journey through the lives of the patriarchs and the tribes, we are reminded of the divine promise that transcends time and circumstance. It is a promise that calls us to trust in God's plan and to walk in the legacy of faith left by those who have gone before us. Through the Twelve Tribes, we see the unfolding of a divine narrative that points us to the ultimate fulfillment of God's promise in Jesus Christ, the Savior of the world.

Chapter 2: Isaac and Jacob

Summary: The narrative continues with Isaac and the birth of Jacob and Esau, emphasizing Jacob's role in God's plan.

Bible Verse: Genesis 25:23 - "The LORD said to her, 'Two nations are in your womb, and two peoples from within you will be separated; one people will be stronger than the other, and the older will serve the younger.'"

The story of Isaac, the child of promise, and his sons, Jacob and Esau, is a profound continuation of the divine narrative initiated with Abraham. It is a tale of faith, struggle, and the unfolding of God's plan through the generations. Isaac's life, though less tumultuous than his father Abraham's, was marked by significant events that shaped the destiny of his descendants. Central to this narrative are his twin sons, Jacob and Esau, whose lives exemplify the complexities of divine election and human agency.

Isaac's birth was nothing short of a miracle. Born to Abraham and Sarah in their old age, Isaac was the fulfillment of God's promise and a testament to His faithfulness. His early years were spent under the protective and nurturing gaze of his parents, who were acutely aware of the divine purpose attached to his life. The joy and laughter his birth brought to his parents were encapsulated in his name, Isaac, meaning "he laughs."

As Isaac grew, he became a living embodiment of the covenant God had made with Abraham. His marriage to Rebekah was a significant event orchestrated by divine providence. Abraham, in his advanced years, sent his trusted servant Eliezer to find a wife for Isaac from his own kin. The journey led Eliezer to Rebekah, a woman of great virtue and beauty, who was willing to leave her family and homeland to marry Isaac. This union was blessed by God, and it set the stage for the next chapter in the unfolding of His promise.

Rebekah's entrance into Isaac's life marked the beginning of a new era. Their marriage was initially marred by Rebekah's barrenness, a trial that tested their faith and patience. For twenty years, Isaac prayed earnestly for his wife, and God answered his prayers, blessing them with twin sons. The pregnancy, however, was tumultuous, with Rebekah experiencing intense discomfort. Seeking God's counsel, she received a prophetic word that would shape the destiny of her children and their descendants: "Two nations are in your womb, and two peoples from within you will be separated; one people will be stronger than the other, and the older will serve the younger" (Genesis 25:23).

This prophecy was a revelation of God's sovereign plan, indicating that the younger son, Jacob, would inherit the promise and play a pivotal role in the unfolding of God's purposes. The birth of the twins was marked by a struggle that symbolized their future relationship. Esau, the firstborn, emerged red and hairy, earning his name, which means "hairy." Jacob, whose name means "he grasps the heel," was born clutching his brother's heel, a foreshadowing of the struggles and conflicts that would characterize their relationship.

As the twins grew, their differences became increasingly apparent. Esau became a skilled hunter, a man of the field, favored by Isaac, who delighted in the game Esau provided. Jacob, in contrast, was a quiet man, dwelling in tents, and was favored by Rebekah. This parental favoritism sowed the seeds of discord and competition between the brothers.

Esau, impulsive and driven by immediate gratification, sold his birthright to Jacob for a bowl of lentil stew. This transaction, seemingly trivial, had profound implications. The birthright, which included leadership of the family and a double portion of the inheritance, was a significant aspect of the covenantal promise. Esau's disdain for his birthright and Jacob's cunning in acquiring it highlighted their contrasting characters and set the stage for future conflicts.

The climactic moment in the brothers' rivalry came with Isaac's blessing. As Isaac aged and his eyesight failed, he decided to bestow his blessing upon Esau. Rebekah, recalling God's prophecy, devised a plan for Jacob to receive the blessing instead. She prepared a meal for Isaac and dressed Jacob in Esau's clothing, covering his hands and neck with goat skins to mimic Esau's hairy texture. The deception succeeded, and Isaac, believing he was blessing Esau, bestowed the blessing upon Jacob, declaring that nations would serve him and that he would be master over his brothers.

When Esau discovered the deception, his anger and sense of betrayal were immense. He vowed to kill Jacob, prompting Rebekah to send Jacob away to her brother Laban in Haran. This departure marked the beginning of Jacob's journey of transformation and growth, a journey that would shape his character and fulfill God's promise.

Jacob's time in Haran was marked by labor, love, and divine encounters. Upon arriving, he met Rachel, Laban's younger daughter, and fell deeply in love with her. He agreed to work for Laban for seven years in exchange for Rachel's hand in marriage. However, on the wedding night, Laban deceived Jacob by substituting Leah, his elder daughter, for Rachel. Jacob's sense of betrayal mirrored his own deception of Isaac and Esau, highlighting the principle of reaping what one sows.

Despite the deception, Jacob worked another seven years for Rachel, solidifying his commitment and love for her. His time with Laban was marked by further challenges and divine blessings. God prospered Jacob, multiplying his flocks and wealth despite Laban's attempts to exploit him. During this period, Jacob fathered twelve sons and one daughter, laying the foundation for the twelve tribes of Israel.

Jacob's departure from Haran was as dramatic as his arrival. Sensing Laban's growing hostility and prompted by God's command, Jacob left secretly with his family and possessions. Laban pursued him, but a divine warning in a dream prevented any harm. A covenant of peace was established between them, and Jacob continued his journey back to Canaan.

The most significant turning point in Jacob's life occurred during his journey home. Fearing Esau's vengeance, Jacob prayed earnestly for God's protection. One night, he found himself wrestling with a mysterious man until daybreak. This encounter was a physical and spiritual struggle, symbolizing Jacob's lifelong struggle with God and men. As dawn broke, the man touched Jacob's hip, dislocating it, and blessed him, giving him a new name, Israel, meaning "he struggles with God."

This divine encounter marked Jacob's transformation. He emerged with a limp, a physical reminder of his encounter with God, but also with a new identity and a renewed sense of purpose. Reconciled with Esau, Jacob returned to Canaan, where he would live out his days as the patriarch of a burgeoning nation.

Jacob's life, marked by struggle, deception, and ultimately transformation, is a profound testament to God's faithfulness and sovereignty. His journey from cunning deceiver to a man of faith mirrors the broader narrative of Israel's journey as a nation. Jacob, now Israel, fathered twelve sons, each of whom would become the progenitor of the twelve tribes of Israel, fulfilling God's promise to Abraham.

Esau, despite losing the birthright and blessing, also prospered and became the ancestor of the Edomites. His life, marked by impulsiveness and reconciliation, serves as a reminder of God's grace and the complexities of human relationships within the framework of divine sovereignty.

The narrative of Isaac, Jacob, and Esau is a rich tapestry of faith, struggle, and divine purpose. It highlights the interplay between human agency and divine election, demonstrating that God's purposes prevail despite human flaws and failures. Isaac's faith, Jacob's transformation, and Esau's reconciliation are all integral parts of the unfolding of God's redemptive plan.

As we reflect on the lives of Isaac, Jacob, and Esau, we are reminded of the profound truth encapsulated in Genesis 25:23: "The LORD said to her, 'Two nations are in your womb, and two peoples from within you will be separated; one people will be stronger than the other, and the older will serve the younger.'" This prophecy, given to Rebekah, set the stage for the unfolding of God's plan through the lives of her sons and their descendants.

The story of Isaac and Jacob is not just an ancient narrative but a living testament to the faithfulness of God and the fulfillment of His promises. It calls us to faith, perseverance, and trust in God's sovereign plan, reminding us that He is faithful to complete the work He begins in us. Through the lives of Isaac, Jacob, and Esau, we see the unfolding of a divine narrative that points us to the ultimate fulfillment of God's promise in Jesus Christ, the Savior of the world.

In the broader context of God's redemptive plan, the story of Isaac and Jacob serves as a pivotal chapter. The birthright and blessing, central themes in their narrative, are more than familial inheritance; they are conduits of God's covenantal promise. This promise, initiated with Abraham, is carried through Isaac and Jacob, each playing a crucial role in its fulfillment.

Isaac's life, though less dramatic than his father Abraham's, was marked by faith and obedience. His experiences, from the binding on Mount Moriah to the wells of Gerar, reflect a steady trust in God's provision and promise. The wells Isaac dug were not just sources of water but symbols of God's ongoing blessing and presence. Each well, contested and reclaimed, represented a reaffirmation of the promise given to Abraham.

Isaac's relationship with his sons, Esau and Jacob, highlights the complexities of parental favoritism and divine election. Isaac's favoritism towards Esau and Rebekah's towards Jacob set the stage for conflict, yet it was within this familial tension that God's purposes unfolded. The sale of Esau's birthright to Jacob, while seemingly a minor event, was a significant turning point, reflecting Esau's disregard for spiritual heritage and Jacob's desire for the blessing.

Jacob's deception in obtaining Isaac's blessing was a culmination of the tensions within the family. Rebekah's role in the deception was motivated by her remembrance of God's prophecy, yet it resulted in profound consequences. Jacob's flight to Haran and his subsequent years of labor under Laban were marked by divine encounters and personal growth. Each trial and blessing Jacob experienced was a step in his transformation from a deceiver to a patriarch.

Jacob's journey back to Canaan was marked by a profound encounter with God at Peniel. The wrestling match, both physical and spiritual, symbolized Jacob's lifelong struggle with God and men. His new name, Israel, signified a new identity and purpose, a transition from self-reliance to reliance on God. This transformation was critical in preparing Jacob to fulfill his role as the father of the twelve tribes.

The reconciliation between Jacob and Esau is a poignant moment in their narrative. Esau's forgiveness and Jacob's humility reflect the possibility of healing and restoration within fractured relationships. Their reunion, marked by tears and embraces, was a testimony to the power of forgiveness and the fulfillment of God's promise to Abraham.

Jacob's later years were marked by the challenges and joys of fatherhood. His twelve sons, each unique in character and destiny, became the progenitors of the twelve tribes of Israel. The favoritism Jacob showed towards Joseph, his beloved son from Rachel, mirrored the favoritism shown by Isaac and Rebekah, leading to further family conflict. Yet, God's providence was evident even in these conflicts, as Joseph's journey from slavery to prominence in Egypt was instrumental in the preservation of the family during famine.

The narrative of Isaac and Jacob is a rich tapestry that weaves together themes of faith, struggle, and divine purpose. It highlights the interplay between human agency and divine sovereignty, demonstrating that God's purposes prevail despite human flaws and failures. Isaac's faith, Jacob's transformation, and Esau's reconciliation are all integral parts of the unfolding of God's redemptive plan.

As we reflect on the lives of Isaac, Jacob, and Esau, we are reminded of the profound truth encapsulated in Genesis 25:23: "The LORD said to her, 'Two nations are in your womb, and two peoples from within you will be separated; one people will be stronger than the other, and the older will serve the younger.'" This prophecy, given to Rebekah, set the stage for the unfolding of God's plan through the lives of her sons and their descendants.

The story of Isaac and Jacob is not just an ancient narrative but a living testament to the faithfulness of God and the fulfillment of His promises. It calls us to faith, perseverance, and trust in God's sovereign plan, reminding us that He is faithful to complete the work He begins in us. Through the lives of Isaac, Jacob, and Esau, we see the unfolding of a divine narrative that points us to the ultimate fulfillment of God's promise in Jesus Christ, the Savior of the world.

The legacy of Isaac and Jacob is one of profound significance in the history of Israel and the overarching narrative of God's redemptive plan. Isaac, the child of promise, and Jacob, the one who wrestled with God, each played pivotal roles in the unfolding of the covenant. Their lives, marked by faith, struggle, and divine encounters, offer timeless lessons on the nature of God's promises and the human response to His call.

Isaac's life was a bridge between the faith of Abraham and the emergence of Israel. His experiences, though less dramatic, were essential in maintaining the continuity of the covenant. The wells he dug, the fields he cultivated, and the altars he built were all acts of faith that kept alive the promise given to his father. His marriage to Rebekah, orchestrated by divine providence, ensured the continuation of the covenantal line.

The birth of Jacob and Esau was a fulfillment of Isaac and Rebekah's prayers, yet it also introduced new dynamics into the family. The prophecy given to Rebekah about her sons foreshadowed the complexities of their relationship and the broader narrative of divine election. Jacob's cunning and Esau's impulsiveness were characteristics that played into the unfolding of God's plan, demonstrating that God works through the complexities and imperfections of human nature.

Jacob's life is a testament to transformation and the power of divine encounter. From his early days of deception to his transformative experience at Bethel and his wrestling with God at Peniel, Jacob's journey was one of significant personal and spiritual growth. His new name, Israel, signified not just a personal transformation but the birth of a nation. The twelve sons he fathered became the foundation of the twelve tribes, each carrying forward the promise given to Abraham.

Esau's story, while often overshadowed by Jacob's, is also significant. His impulsive decision to sell his birthright and his eventual reconciliation with Jacob highlight themes of regret, forgiveness, and grace. Esau's descendants, the Edomites, played their own role in the broader narrative of Israel, demonstrating that God's purposes extend beyond individual lives to encompass entire nations.

The narrative of Isaac and Jacob is a rich tapestry of faith, struggle, and divine purpose. It highlights the interplay between human agency and divine sovereignty, demonstrating that God's purposes prevail despite human flaws and failures. Isaac's faith, Jacob's transformation, and Esau's reconciliation are all integral parts of the unfolding of God's redemptive plan.

As we reflect on the lives of Isaac, Jacob, and Esau, we are reminded of the profound truth encapsulated in Genesis 25:23: "The LORD said to her, 'Two nations are in your womb, and two peoples from within you will be separated; one people will be stronger than the other, and the older will serve the younger.'" This prophecy, given to Rebekah, set the stage for the unfolding of God's plan through the lives of her sons and their descendants.

The story of Isaac and Jacob is not just an ancient narrative but a living testament to the faithfulness of God and the fulfillment of His promises. It calls us to faith, perseverance, and trust in God's sovereign plan, reminding us that He is faithful to complete the work He begins in us. Through the lives of Isaac, Jacob, and Esau, we see the unfolding of a divine narrative that points us to the ultimate fulfillment of God's promise in Jesus Christ, the Savior of the world.

The story of Isaac and Jacob is not just an ancient narrative but a living testament to the faithfulness of God and the fulfillment of His promises. It calls us to faith, perseverance, and trust in God's sovereign plan, reminding us that He is faithful to complete the work He begins in us. Through the lives of Isaac, Jacob, and Esau, we see the unfolding of a divine narrative that points us to the ultimate fulfillment of God's promise in Jesus Christ, the Savior of the world.

Bible Verse: Genesis 25:23 - "The LORD said to her, 'Two nations are in your womb, and two peoples from within you will be separated; one people will be stronger than the other, and the older will serve the younger.'"

This verse encapsulates the divine purpose and plan that unfolded through the lives of Isaac, Jacob, and Esau. It is a reminder that God's promises are sure and that His purposes will prevail, regardless of human frailty and failure. As we continue to explore the narrative of the twelve tribes, we are called to reflect on our own journey of faith and trust in the God who is faithful to fulfill His promises.

Chapter 3: Jacob's Ladder

Summary: Jacob's vision at Bethel, where God reaffirms the covenant made with Abraham.

Bible Verse: Genesis 28:13-14 - "There above it stood the LORD, and he said: 'I am the LORD, the God of your father Abraham and the God of Isaac. I will give you and your descendants the land on which you are lying. Your descendants will be like the dust of the earth.'"

The story of Jacob, the third patriarch of Israel, is marked by a series of divine encounters and personal transformations that not only shaped his destiny but also reaffirmed the covenant God made with his grandfather Abraham and his father Isaac. One of the most profound of these encounters occurred at Bethel, a place that became synonymous with divine revelation and the reaffirmation of God's promises. This chapter delves into the significance of Jacob's vision at Bethel, exploring its theological, historical, and personal implications.

Jacob's journey to Bethel was precipitated by familial conflict and divine destiny. Having deceived his father Isaac and cheated his brother Esau out of both his birthright and blessing, Jacob was forced to flee for his life. Esau's anger was palpable, and Rebekah, aware of the danger, urged Jacob to seek refuge with her brother Laban in Haran. This journey, fraught with uncertainty and fear, marked the beginning of a new chapter in Jacob's life, one that would be defined by divine encounters and transformative experiences.

As Jacob left Beersheba and set out for Haran, he found himself alone in the wilderness. The journey was long and arduous, filled with the unknown. It was in this setting, with the weight of his actions and the fear of the future pressing upon him, that Jacob experienced one of the most significant divine encounters recorded in the Scriptures. As the sun set and darkness enveloped the landscape, Jacob found a place to rest. Using a stone for a pillow, he lay down to sleep, and it was during this sleep that God revealed Himself to Jacob in a dream.

In the dream, Jacob saw a ladder, or staircase, resting on the earth with its top reaching to heaven. The angels of God were ascending and descending on it, symbolizing the connection between the divine and the earthly realms.

This vision was a powerful reminder of God's presence and His ongoing involvement in the world. At the top of the ladder stood the Lord, who spoke to Jacob, reaffirming the covenant made with Abraham and Isaac: "I am the LORD, the God of your father Abraham and the God of Isaac. I will give you and your descendants the land on which you are lying. Your descendants will be like the dust of the earth, and you will spread out to the west and to the east, to the north and to the south. All peoples on earth will be blessed through you and your offspring" (Genesis 28:13-14).

This divine declaration was not merely a repetition of promises made to Jacob's forebears but a personal reaffirmation to Jacob himself. Despite his deceptive actions and the turmoil in his life, God's promise remained steadfast. The vision of the ladder, with angels ascending and descending, underscored the accessibility of divine grace and the continuous interaction between heaven and earth. It was a reminder that God's presence and His promises transcended human failings and were rooted in His sovereign will.

Jacob awoke from his sleep with a profound sense of awe and reverence. He exclaimed, "Surely the LORD is in this place, and I was not aware of it. How awesome is this place! This is none other than the house of God; this is the gate of heaven" (Genesis 28:16-17). This recognition marked a turning point in Jacob's spiritual journey. The place where he had slept was no ordinary location; it was Bethel, meaning "house of God," a sacred space where heaven and earth intersected.

In response to the divine encounter, Jacob took the stone he had used as a pillow and set it up as a pillar, pouring oil on top of it. This act of anointing the stone was a way of consecrating the place and marking it as holy. Jacob then made a vow, saying, "If God will be with me and will watch over me on this journey I am taking and will give me food to eat and clothes to wear so that I return safely to my father's household, then the LORD will be my God and this stone that I have set up as a pillar will be God's house, and of all that you give me I will give you a tenth" (Genesis 28:20-22).

Jacob's vow reflected his deep desire for God's guidance and protection. It was an acknowledgment of his dependence on divine provision and a commitment to honor God with his life and resources. The vow also highlighted Jacob's growing awareness of God's presence and his emerging faith in the covenant promises.

The vision at Bethel was a pivotal moment in Jacob's life, but it was also significant in the broader narrative of Israel's history. Bethel became a central location in the spiritual life of the nation, a place where God's presence was profoundly felt and His promises reaffirmed. Throughout the generations, Bethel would be a site of worship and encounter, a reminder of God's faithfulness to His covenant people.

Jacob's journey continued, and as he traveled to Haran, the memory of Bethel remained a source of encouragement and strength. In Haran, Jacob faced new challenges and opportunities that would further shape his character and destiny. His time with Laban was marked by hard labor, love, and divine blessing. Jacob fell in love with Rachel, Laban's younger daughter, and agreed to work for seven years to marry her. However, Laban deceived him, substituting Leah, Rachel's elder sister, on the wedding night. Jacob's sense of betrayal mirrored his own deceptive actions earlier in life, underscoring the principle of reaping what one sows.

Despite the deception, Jacob's love for Rachel remained steadfast, and he agreed to work another seven years for her. During his time in Haran, God continued to bless Jacob, multiplying his flocks and increasing his wealth. Jacob's experiences in Haran were a time of growth and refinement, preparing him for his eventual return to Canaan and the fulfillment of God's promises.

Jacob's departure from Haran was marked by divine instruction and protection. Sensing Laban's growing hostility and prompted by God's command, Jacob left secretly with his family and possessions. Laban pursued him, but a divine warning in a dream prevented any harm. A covenant of peace was established between them, and Jacob continued his journey back to Canaan.

The journey back to Canaan was fraught with anticipation and fear. Jacob remembered the anger of his brother Esau and feared for his life and the lives of his family. In this time of distress, Jacob sought God's guidance and protection, praying earnestly for deliverance. His prayer was a heartfelt plea for mercy, reflecting his deep dependence on God's grace.

One of the most significant moments in Jacob's journey back to Canaan occurred when he was left alone one night. A man appeared and wrestled with Jacob until daybreak. This mysterious encounter was both physical and spiritual, symbolizing Jacob's lifelong struggle with God and men. As dawn broke, the man touched Jacob's hip, dislocating it, and blessed him, giving him a new name, Israel, meaning "he struggles with God." This divine encounter marked Jacob's transformation, solidifying his identity and purpose as the father of the twelve tribes of Israel.

Jacob's reconciliation with Esau was a poignant moment of grace and forgiveness. Esau's forgiveness and Jacob's humility reflected the possibility of healing and restoration within fractured relationships. Their reunion, marked by tears and embraces, was a testimony to the power of forgiveness and the fulfillment of God's promise to Abraham.

As Jacob settled in Canaan, he remembered the vow he had made at Bethel. He returned to Bethel, where he built an altar and called the place El-Bethel, meaning "God of Bethel." This act of worship and remembrance was a reaffirmation of Jacob's faith and commitment to the God who had been with him throughout his journey.

The vision at Bethel and Jacob's subsequent experiences highlight the interplay between divine sovereignty and human agency. Jacob's life, marked by deception, struggle, and ultimately transformation, is a testament to God's faithfulness and the fulfillment of His promises. Despite Jacob's flaws and failures, God's purposes prevailed, underscoring the truth that divine grace is greater than human weakness.

Jacob's vision at Bethel also foreshadows the greater fulfillment of God's promise in Jesus Christ. The ladder connecting heaven and earth is a symbol of Christ, the mediator between God and humanity. Through Christ, the promises made to Abraham, Isaac, and Jacob find their ultimate fulfillment, bringing salvation and blessing to all nations.

The story of Jacob's ladder is not just an ancient narrative but a living testament to the faithfulness of God and the fulfillment of His promises. It calls us to faith, perseverance, and trust in God's sovereign plan, reminding us that He is faithful to complete the work He begins in us. Through the lives of the patriarchs, we see the unfolding of a divine narrative that points us to the ultimate fulfillment of God's promise in Jesus Christ, the Savior of the world.

As we delve deeper into the story of Jacob's ladder, it is essential to understand its theological significance and how it fits into the larger biblical narrative. The vision of the ladder or staircase connecting heaven and earth serves as a powerful metaphor for the relationship between the divine and the human, and it reveals profound truths about God's nature and His interaction with His creation.

The imagery of the ladder itself is rich with meaning. In the ancient Near Eastern context, ziggurats, or stepped pyramids, were often seen as connecting points between heaven and earth, where the gods could descend to interact with humanity. Jacob's vision reinterprets this imagery within the framework of monotheism, presenting the true God, Yahweh, as the one who bridges the gap between heaven and earth. The angels ascending and descending the ladder represent God's ongoing activity and involvement in the world, carrying out His will and serving as messengers between the divine and human realms.

At the top of the ladder stands the Lord, who identifies Himself as the God of Abraham and Isaac. This introduction is significant because it ties Jacob's vision directly to the covenantal promises made to his forefathers. God's reaffirmation of these promises to Jacob underscores the continuity of His plan and the unchanging nature of His covenant. Despite human failings and the passage of time, God's promises remain steadfast.

The content of God's promise to Jacob at Bethel mirrors the earlier promises made to Abraham and Isaac: "I will give you and your descendants the land on which you are lying. Your descendants will be like the dust of the earth, and you will spread out to the west and to the east, to the north and to the south. All peoples on earth will be blessed through you and your offspring" (Genesis 28:13-14). This promise includes three key elements: land, descendants, and blessing. Each element is crucial in understanding the scope of God's covenant.

The promise of land signifies God's provision and the establishment of a place where His people can dwell and flourish. It is a tangible sign of God's faithfulness and a foretaste of the ultimate inheritance that awaits His people. For Jacob, the land of Canaan was a physical reminder of God's promise and a place where he and his descendants would experience God's blessings.

The promise of numerous descendants highlights God's ability to bring life and fruitfulness where there was barrenness. For a man who had fled his homeland and was uncertain about his future, this promise was a powerful assurance of God's continued blessing and provision. Jacob's descendants, the twelve tribes of Israel, would become a great nation, fulfilling God's promise and playing a pivotal role in His redemptive plan.

The promise that "all peoples on earth will be blessed through you and your offspring" points to the universal scope of God's covenant. It is a foreshadowing of the Messiah, Jesus Christ, through whom all nations would indeed be blessed. This element of the promise transcends the immediate context of Jacob's life and points to the ultimate fulfillment of God's redemptive purposes in Christ.

Jacob's response to the vision at Bethel reflects his growing faith and awareness of God's presence. His exclamation, "Surely the LORD is in this place, and I was not aware of it," indicates a profound recognition of the sacredness of the moment and the place. Jacob's act of setting up the stone as a pillar and anointing it with oil was a way of consecrating the place and marking it as holy. This act of worship was a tangible expression of his reverence and commitment to the God who had revealed Himself to him.

The vow Jacob made at Bethel is also significant. It reflects his desire for God's guidance and protection on his journey and his commitment to serve the Lord. Jacob's vow to give a tenth of all that God gave him was an acknowledgment of God's provision and a pledge of his dedication to the covenant. This act of tithing was a precursor to the later practice in Israelite worship and underscored the principle of honoring God with one's resources.

Jacob's vision at Bethel was a pivotal moment that shaped his identity and destiny. It was a reminder of God's faithfulness and a call to trust in His promises. As Jacob continued his journey, the memory of Bethel remained a source of strength and encouragement. In Haran, despite the challenges and deceptions he faced, Jacob experienced God's blessing and provision, reaffirming the promise made at Bethel.

The return to Bethel later in Jacob's life was a significant act of worship and remembrance. By building an altar and calling the place El-Bethel, Jacob reaffirmed his commitment to the God who had been with him throughout his journey. This act of worship was not only a personal declaration of faith but also a testimony to his family and future generations of God's faithfulness.

The theological significance of Jacob's ladder extends beyond the immediate context of Jacob's life. In the New Testament, Jesus references this vision in His conversation with Nathanael: "Very truly I tell you, you will see 'heaven open, and the angels of God ascending and descending on' the Son of Man" (John 1:51). Jesus identifies Himself as the true ladder, the bridge between heaven and earth. Through His incarnation, death, and resurrection, Jesus becomes the mediator who connects humanity with God, fulfilling the promise of blessing to all nations.

Jacob's vision at Bethel thus serves as a foreshadowing of the greater fulfillment of God's promise in Christ. It points to the ultimate reconciliation between God and humanity and the establishment of God's kingdom on earth. Through Jesus, the promises made to Abraham, Isaac, and Jacob find their ultimate fulfillment, bringing salvation and blessing to all who believe.

The story of Jacob's ladder is a rich and profound narrative that speaks to the enduring faithfulness of God and the unfolding of His redemptive plan. It calls us to faith, perseverance, and trust in God's promises, reminding us that He is faithful to complete the work He begins in us. Through the lives of the patriarchs, we see the divine narrative that points us to the ultimate fulfillment of God's promise in Jesus Christ, the Savior of the world.

The vision at Bethel and its implications for Jacob's life and the broader biblical narrative offer profound insights into the nature of God's covenant and His interaction with humanity. As we continue to explore the significance of this divine encounter, it is essential to consider the personal, historical, and theological dimensions of Jacob's experience and how they resonate with our understanding of God's faithfulness and His redemptive purposes.

On a personal level, Jacob's vision at Bethel was a transformative experience that marked a turning point in his spiritual journey. Prior to this encounter, Jacob's actions were driven by self-interest and deception. His acquisition of Esau's birthright and his deceitful receipt of Isaac's blessing were indicative of his reliance on cunning and manipulation. However, the vision at Bethel confronted Jacob with the reality of God's presence and the seriousness of the covenantal promises.

Jacob's reaction to the vision—his fear, awe, and subsequent vow—indicates a shift in his understanding of God and his role in the divine plan. The acknowledgment that "Surely the LORD is in this place, and I was not aware of it" reflects Jacob's awakening to the omnipresence of God. This realization was a catalyst for his transformation, moving him from a life of deception to one of faith and dependence on God's guidance.

Historically, Bethel became a significant location in the narrative of Israel. It was not only the site of Jacob's vision but also a place of worship and encounter for future generations. The name Bethel, meaning "house of God," signifies its importance as a sacred space where God's presence was manifest. Throughout Israel's history, Bethel remained a place of pilgrimage and worship, a reminder of the foundational promises made to the patriarchs.

Theologically, Jacob's vision at Bethel encapsulates the essence of the covenantal relationship between God and His people. The ladder, with angels ascending and descending, symbolizes the connection between heaven and earth and the accessibility of divine grace. God's reaffirmation of the promises to Jacob underscores the continuity of His covenant and His unchanging nature. Despite human flaws and failures, God's purposes prevail, and His promises are fulfilled.

The promise of land, descendants, and blessing given to Jacob at Bethel is a reiteration of the earlier covenantal promises made to Abraham and Isaac. Each element of this promise carries profound theological significance. The land represents God's provision and the establishment of a place where His people can dwell and flourish. The descendants signify the fruitfulness and continuity of God's covenantal relationship. The promise of blessing to all nations points to the universal scope of God's redemptive plan, culminating in the person and work of Jesus Christ.

Jacob's vow in response to the vision reflects his growing faith and commitment to the covenant. His promise to give a tenth of all that God gives him is an acknowledgment of divine provision and a pledge of dedication to God. This act of tithing, later formalized in the Mosaic Law, underscores the principle of honoring God with one's resources and recognizing His sovereignty over all aspects of life.

The vision at Bethel also has eschatological implications, pointing to the ultimate fulfillment of God's promises in Christ. Jesus, as the true ladder, bridges the gap between heaven and earth, offering reconciliation and redemption to humanity. Through His life, death, and resurrection, Jesus fulfills the promise of blessing to all nations, inaugurating the kingdom of God and establishing a new covenant.

Jacob's journey, marked by divine encounters and personal transformation, is a microcosm of the broader narrative of Israel and God's redemptive purposes. His experiences reflect the complexities of human agency and divine sovereignty, demonstrating that God's purposes prevail despite human failings.

The vision at Bethel is a testament to God's faithfulness and the enduring nature of His covenant, calling us to trust in His promises and walk in the legacy of faith.

As we reflect on the significance of Jacob's ladder, we are reminded of the profound truth encapsulated in Genesis 28:13-14: "There above it stood the LORD, and he said: 'I am the LORD, the God of your father Abraham and the God of Isaac. I will give you and your descendants the land on which you are lying. Your descendants will be like the dust of the earth.'" This divine declaration is a testament to God's faithfulness and a call to trust in His sovereign plan.

Jacob's vision at Bethel, with its rich theological, historical, and personal dimensions, offers a profound insight into the nature of God's covenant and His interaction with humanity. It is a narrative that calls us to faith, perseverance, and trust in God's promises, reminding us that He is faithful to complete the work He begins in us. Through the lives of the patriarchs, we see the unfolding of a divine narrative that points us to the ultimate fulfillment of God's promise in Jesus Christ, the Savior of the world.

Chapter 4: The Twelve Sons

Summary: The chapter details the birth of Jacob's twelve sons, who become the patriarchs of the Twelve Tribes.

Bible Verse: Genesis 35:22b - "Jacob had twelve sons."

The story of Jacob's twelve sons, who would become the patriarchs of the Twelve Tribes of Israel, is one of the most pivotal in the history of the Israelites. These twelve sons were not just individual figures; they collectively formed the foundation of the nation of Israel. Each son's birth, life, and descendants played a crucial role in fulfilling the covenantal promises made by God to Abraham, Isaac, and Jacob. This chapter explores the lives of these twelve sons, their significance, and their lasting legacy in the biblical narrative.

Jacob, later named Israel after his transformative encounter with God, had twelve sons through his wives Leah and Rachel and their maidservants, Zilpah and Bilhah. The births of these sons occurred during Jacob's long sojourn in Haran, where he served his uncle Laban. This period was marked by a mix of personal strife, divine blessing, and prophetic significance.

The Sons of Leah

Reuben

Reuben was Jacob's firstborn son, born to Leah. His birth is recorded in Genesis 29:32, where Leah named him Reuben, meaning "See, a son," because she believed that God had noticed her misery and blessed her with a child. As the firstborn, Reuben held a special place in the family, with the rights and responsibilities that came with the birthright. However, Reuben's later actions, particularly his indiscretion with Bilhah, his father's concubine, led to the loss of his preeminent status. This incident, mentioned in Genesis 35:22, had long-lasting consequences, affecting Reuben's standing and the future of his descendants.

Despite this, Reuben's descendants formed one of the tribes of Israel. The tribe of Reuben settled on the east side of the Jordan River, a fertile area conducive to their lifestyle. The tribe played a significant role during the early years of Israel's formation and conquest of Canaan, although they struggled with maintaining their position among the other tribes due to Reuben's past actions.

Simeon and Levi

Simeon and Levi were the second and third sons of Jacob and Leah. Their births are recorded in Genesis 29:33-34. Simeon's name means "one who hears," reflecting Leah's belief that God had heard her prayers. Levi's name means "attached" or "joined," symbolizing Leah's hope that Jacob would become more attached to her.

Simeon and Levi are often remembered for their fierce and violent reaction to the defilement of their sister Dinah by Shechem, a prince of the land. In Genesis 34, Simeon and Levi took matters into their own hands, deceiving Shechem and his people and then attacking and killing all the males in the city. This act of vengeance, while defending their sister's honor, also brought Jacob's reproach and had significant implications for their descendants.

The tribe of Simeon eventually became one of the lesser tribes, with their territory mostly absorbed into the land of Judah. In contrast, the tribe of Levi was set apart for religious duties. Levi's descendants became the Levitical priests, serving in the Tabernacle and later in the Temple. This special role was a significant transformation from their ancestral actions, showing God's ability to redeem and repurpose.

Judah

Judah, Leah's fourth son, holds a particularly prominent place in the biblical narrative. His birth is recorded in Genesis 29:35, where Leah names him Judah, meaning "praise." Judah's significance extends beyond his personal actions to the future of Israel and the lineage of the Messiah.

Judah emerged as a leader among his brothers, particularly in the story of Joseph. When Joseph was sold into slavery by his brothers, it was Judah who later took responsibility, offering himself as a surety for Benjamin when they had to return to Egypt. Judah's leadership and willingness to act for the greater good of the family earned him a prominent role.

The tribe of Judah became one of the most powerful and influential tribes in Israel. It was from Judah's line that King David emerged, and ultimately, Jesus Christ, fulfilling the messianic prophecies. Judah's blessing from Jacob, recorded in Genesis 49:8-12, speaks of a lion's strength and a ruler's scepter, indicating the future leadership and kingship that would come from his lineage.

Issachar and Zebulun

Issachar and Zebulun were Leah's fifth and sixth sons. Issachar's birth is recorded in Genesis 30:17-18, where Leah names him Issachar, meaning "reward," reflecting her belief that God had rewarded her for giving her maidservant Zilpah to Jacob. Zebulun's birth is recorded in Genesis 30:19-20, where Leah names him Zebulun, meaning "dwelling," expressing her hope that Jacob would now dwell with her.

Issachar's descendants became known for their wisdom and understanding of the times, as noted in 1 Chronicles 12:32. The tribe of Issachar settled in a fertile region, conducive to agriculture, and played a significant role in supporting the other tribes with their insights and counsel.

Zebulun's descendants settled in the northern region of Israel, near the sea. The tribe of Zebulun became known for their maritime activities and trade, contributing to the economic strength of Israel. Jacob's blessing to Zebulun in Genesis 49:13 speaks of his dwelling by the sea and being a haven for ships, indicating their future prosperity and role in commerce.

The Sons of Rachel

Joseph

Joseph, the firstborn son of Rachel, holds a central place in the narrative of Genesis. His birth is recorded in Genesis 30:22-24, where Rachel names him Joseph, meaning "may he add," expressing her hope for another son. Joseph's life was marked by dreams, favoritism, betrayal, and eventual rise to power in Egypt.

Joseph's dreams, which foretold his future prominence, fueled the jealousy and resentment of his brothers. Their betrayal, selling Joseph into slavery, led to a series of events that ultimately positioned Joseph as a powerful leader in Egypt, second only to Pharaoh. Joseph's wisdom and administrative skills during the years of famine not only saved Egypt but also his own family, leading to the eventual migration of Jacob and his family to Egypt.

Joseph's descendants formed the tribes of Ephraim and Manasseh, named after his two sons. These tribes played significant roles in the history of Israel, particularly Ephraim, which became one of the leading tribes in the northern kingdom. Joseph's blessing from Jacob, recorded in Genesis 49:22-26, speaks of fruitfulness, strength, and divine favor, reflecting his life's journey and impact.

Benjamin

Benjamin, Rachel's second son, was born under tragic circumstances, as Rachel died during childbirth. His birth is recorded in Genesis 35:16-18, where Rachel names him Ben-Oni, meaning "son of my sorrow," but Jacob renames him Benjamin, meaning "son of my right hand." Benjamin's birth marked the completion of the twelve sons of Jacob.

The tribe of Benjamin became known for their bravery and skill in battle. Despite their small size, the Benjaminites played crucial roles in Israel's military and political history. King Saul, Israel's first king, came from the tribe of Benjamin, highlighting their significant contributions to the nation's leadership.

The Sons of Bilhah and Zilpah

Dan and Naphtali

Dan and Naphtali were the sons of Bilhah, Rachel's maidservant. Dan's birth is recorded in Genesis 30:4-6, where Rachel names him Dan, meaning "he judged," reflecting her belief that God had judged her case and granted her a son. Naphtali's birth is recorded in Genesis 30:7-8, where Rachel names him Naphtali, meaning "my struggle," expressing her struggle with her sister Leah.

The tribe of Dan settled in the northern region of Israel and became known for their adventurous and sometimes tumultuous history. The Danites struggled to maintain their territory and often clashed with their neighbors. However, they were also known for their strength and resilience, as reflected in Samson, one of the judges of Israel, who was from the tribe of Dan.

Naphtali's descendants settled in the northern area near the Sea of Galilee. The tribe of Naphtali became known for their swiftness and valor, as noted in Jacob's blessing in Genesis 49:21. They played significant roles in various battles and were noted for their loyalty and dedication to the nation of Israel.

Gad and Asher

Gad and Asher were the sons of Zilpah, Leah's maidservant. Gad's birth is recorded in Genesis 30:9-11, where Leah names him Gad, meaning "good fortune," reflecting her belief in the good fortune that had come to her. Asher's birth is recorded in Genesis 30:12-13, where Leah names him Asher, meaning "happy," expressing her happiness and joy.

The tribe of Gad settled on the east side of the Jordan River, alongside the tribe of Reuben. Gadites were known for their warrior spirit and played crucial roles in defending Israel's territories. They were also instrumental in helping their fellow tribes during times of conflict, displaying loyalty and bravery.

Asher's descendants settled in the fertile regions along the Mediterranean coast. The tribe of Asher became known for their prosperity and abundance, particularly in agricultural produce. Jacob's blessing to Asher in Genesis 49:20 speaks of rich food and royal delicacies, indicating their future prosperity and contribution to Israel's wealth.

Legacy and Significance

The twelve sons of Jacob, despite their diverse backgrounds and varying fortunes, collectively formed the foundation of the nation of Israel. Each son's life and descendants played a crucial role in fulfilling the covenantal promises made by God. The twelve tribes, named after these sons, each had unique characteristics and contributions that enriched the nation.

The blessings Jacob pronounced on his sons before his death, recorded in Genesis 49, reflect both their individual traits and their future roles in Israel's history. These blessings, prophetic in nature, provided insights into the destinies of each tribe and underscored the divine orchestration of Israel's formation.

Jacob's Prophetic Blessings

Before his death, Jacob gathered his twelve sons to bless them and prophesy about their futures. These blessings, recorded in Genesis 49, provide a rich tapestry of prophetic insights into the destinies of the twelve tribes. Each blessing reflects the unique characteristics and future roles of Jacob's sons and their descendants.

Reuben

Jacob's blessing to Reuben reflects both his potential and his failure: "Reuben, you are my firstborn, my might, the first sign of my strength, excelling in honor, excelling in power. Turbulent as the waters, you will no longer excel, for you went up onto your father's bed, onto my couch and defiled it" (Genesis 49:3-4). Reuben's indiscretion cost him his preeminent status, and his descendants struggled to maintain their position among the tribes.

Simeon and Levi

Jacob's words to Simeon and Levi highlight their fierce and violent actions: "Simeon and Levi are brothers—their swords are weapons of violence. Let me not enter their council, let me not join their assembly, for they have killed men in their anger and hamstrung oxen as they pleased. Cursed be their anger, so fierce, and their fury, so cruel! I will scatter them in Jacob and disperse them in Israel" (Genesis 49:5-7). This prophecy foretold their dispersion among the tribes, with Levi's descendants later being set apart for priestly duties.

Judah

Judah's blessing is one of prominence and leadership: "Judah, your brothers will praise you; your hand will be on the neck of your enemies; your father's sons will bow down to you. You are a lion's cub, Judah; you return from the prey, my son. Like a lion he crouches and lies down, like a lioness—who dares to rouse him? The scepter will not depart from Judah, nor the ruler's staff from between his feet, until he to whom it belongs shall come and the obedience of the nations shall be his" (Genesis 49:8-10). This prophecy points to the future kingship from Judah's line, culminating in the Messiah, Jesus Christ.

Zebulun

Jacob's blessing to Zebulun speaks of his future dwelling by the sea: "Zebulun will live by the seashore and become a haven for ships; his border will extend toward Sidon" (Genesis 49:13). Zebulun's descendants became known for their maritime activities and trade, contributing to Israel's economic strength.

Issachar

Issachar's blessing reflects his role as a hardworking and peaceful tribe: "Issachar is a rawboned donkey lying down among the sheep pens. When he sees how good is his resting place and how pleasant is his land, he will bend his shoulder to the burden and submit to forced labor" (Genesis 49:14-15). Issachar's descendants were known for their wisdom and understanding, supporting the other tribes with their insights.

Dan

Jacob's blessing to Dan highlights his role as a judge: "Dan will provide justice for his people as one of the tribes of Israel. Dan will be a snake by the roadside, a viper along the path, that bites the horse's heels so that its rider tumbles backward" (Genesis 49:16-17). The tribe of Dan faced challenges in maintaining their territory but were known for their strength and resilience.

Gad

Gad's blessing speaks of his warrior spirit: "Gad will be attacked by a band of raiders, but he will attack them at their heels" (Genesis 49:19). Gad's descendants were known for their bravery and played crucial roles in defending Israel's territories.

Asher

Asher's blessing reflects his prosperity: "Asher's food will be rich; he will provide delicacies fit for a king" (Genesis 49:20). The tribe of Asher became known for their agricultural abundance and contributed to Israel's wealth.

Naphtali

Jacob's blessing to Naphtali speaks of his swiftness and eloquence: "Naphtali is a doe set free that bears beautiful fawns" (Genesis 49:21). Naphtali's descendants were known for their valor and loyalty, playing significant roles in Israel's history.

Joseph

Joseph's blessing is one of fruitfulness and strength: "Joseph is a fruitful vine, a fruitful vine near a spring, whose branches climb over a wall. With bitterness archers attacked him; they shot at him with hostility. But his bow remained steady, his strong arms stayed limber, because of the hand of the Mighty One of Jacob, because of the Shepherd, the Rock of Israel, because of your father's God, who helps you, because of the Almighty, who blesses you with blessings of the skies above, blessings of the deep springs below, blessings of the breast and womb. Your father's blessings are greater than the blessings of the ancient mountains, than the bounty of the age-old hills. Let all these rest on the head of Joseph, on the brow of the prince among his brothers" (Genesis 49:22-26). Joseph's descendants, Ephraim and Manasseh, played significant roles in Israel's history, with Ephraim becoming a leading tribe in the northern kingdom.

Benjamin

Benjamin's blessing highlights his warrior nature: "Benjamin is a ravenous wolf; in the morning he devours the prey, in the evening he divides the plunder" (Genesis 49:27). The tribe of Benjamin became known for their bravery and skill in battle, contributing to Israel's military strength.

Conclusion

The twelve sons of Jacob, despite their diverse backgrounds and varying fortunes, collectively formed the foundation of the nation of Israel. Each son's life and descendants played a crucial role in fulfilling the covenantal promises made by God. The twelve tribes, named after these sons, each had unique characteristics and contributions that enriched the nation.

The blessings Jacob pronounced on his sons before his death, recorded in Genesis 49, reflect both their individual traits and their future roles in Israel's history. These blessings, prophetic in nature, provided insights into the destinies of each tribe and underscored the divine orchestration of Israel's formation.

Jacob's twelve sons were not just patriarchs of the twelve tribes; they were the embodiment of the covenant promises made by God to Abraham, Isaac, and Jacob. Their lives and descendants reflect the complexities of human nature and the overarching faithfulness of God. Despite their flaws and failures, God's purposes prevailed, leading to the formation of a great nation through which all the peoples of the earth would be blessed.

The legacy of Jacob's twelve sons is a testament to God's enduring faithfulness and His sovereign plan. Their stories, recorded in the Scriptures, continue to inspire and instruct, reminding us of the importance of faith, obedience, and the fulfillment of God's promises. Through the lives of these patriarchs, we see the unfolding of a divine narrative that points to the ultimate fulfillment of God's promise in Jesus Christ, the Savior of the world.

Chapter 5: Joseph and His Brothers

Summary: Focus on Joseph's story, his betrayal by his brothers, and eventual rise to power in Egypt.

Bible Verse: Genesis 50:20 - "You intended to harm me, but God intended it for good to accomplish what is now being done, the saving of many lives."

The story of Joseph and his brothers is one of the most compelling narratives in the Bible, illustrating themes of betrayal, suffering, redemption, and divine providence. Joseph's journey from favored son to slave to ruler of Egypt is a powerful testimony of God's sovereignty and the fulfillment of His purposes despite human intentions. This chapter delves into the complexities of Joseph's relationships with his brothers, his trials and triumphs, and the overarching theme of God's redemptive plan.

Early Life and Family Dynamics

Joseph was the eleventh son of Jacob, born to Rachel, Jacob's beloved wife. From the beginning, Joseph was favored by his father, which created a significant rift between him and his older brothers. This favoritism was symbolized by the ornate coat Jacob gave Joseph, often referred to as the "coat of many colors." This gift not only marked Joseph as Jacob's favorite but also set him apart in a way that incited jealousy and resentment among his brothers.

The family dynamics were further complicated by Joseph's dreams, which he naively shared with his brothers. In one dream, Joseph saw sheaves of grain in the field, with his brothers' sheaves bowing down to his. In another dream, the sun, moon, and eleven stars bowed down to him. These dreams, indicating Joseph's future prominence, fueled his brothers' envy and hatred. They could not accept the idea of bowing to their younger brother, and their resentment grew into a desire to rid themselves of him.

Betrayal and Slavery

The opportunity for betrayal came when Jacob sent Joseph to check on his brothers, who were grazing their flocks near Shechem. As Joseph approached, his brothers saw him from a distance and conspired to kill him. Reuben, the eldest, intervened, suggesting they throw Joseph into a cistern instead, intending to rescue him later. However, when Reuben was away, the brothers sold Joseph to a caravan of Ishmaelites heading to Egypt for twenty pieces of silver.

Joseph's journey to Egypt marked the beginning of a series of trials that would test his faith and character. Sold as a slave to Potiphar, the captain of Pharaoh's guard, Joseph faced a drastic change in status. Despite his circumstances, Joseph excelled in his duties, and Potiphar recognized his abilities, putting him in charge of his household. The Bible records that "the LORD was with Joseph so that he prospered, and he lived in the house of his Egyptian master" (Genesis 39:2).

Temptation and Imprisonment

Joseph's integrity and dedication, however, attracted the attention of Potiphar's wife, who attempted to seduce him. Joseph resisted her advances, stating, "How then could I do such a wicked thing and sin against God?" (Genesis 39:9). Despite his refusal, Potiphar's wife falsely accused him of attempting to rape her, leading to Joseph's imprisonment.

In prison, Joseph continued to exhibit remarkable faith and resilience. His leadership skills and integrity were recognized by the prison warden, who put him in charge of all the prisoners. The Bible notes, "The warden paid no attention to anything under Joseph's care, because the LORD was with Joseph and gave him success in whatever he did" (Genesis 39:23).

Interpretation of Dreams

While in prison, Joseph encountered Pharaoh's cupbearer and baker, both of whom had been imprisoned for offending their master. They each had troubling dreams, and Joseph, through God's guidance, interpreted them. The cupbearer's dream foretold his restoration to Pharaoh's service, while the baker's dream predicted his execution. Joseph's interpretations proved accurate, and the cupbearer was restored to his position.

Joseph requested the cupbearer to remember him and mention him to Pharaoh, but the cupbearer forgot Joseph for two more years. This period of waiting and uncertainty further tested Joseph's faith, yet it also set the stage for his eventual rise to power.

Rise to Power

Pharaoh himself had two troubling dreams that none of his magicians or wise men could interpret. The cupbearer then remembered Joseph and his ability to interpret dreams, and Pharaoh summoned Joseph from the prison. Joseph interpreted Pharaoh's dreams as a divine revelation of seven years of abundance followed by seven years of severe famine. He advised Pharaoh to appoint a wise and discerning man to oversee the storage of surplus grain during the years of abundance to prepare for the famine.

Impressed by Joseph's wisdom and recognizing the Spirit of God in him, Pharaoh appointed Joseph as his second-in-command, saying, "You shall be in charge of my palace, and all my people are to submit to your orders. Only with respect to the throne will I be greater than you" (Genesis 41:40). Joseph was given the Egyptian name Zaphenath-Paneah and married Asenath, the daughter of Potiphera, priest of On. Joseph's rise to power was remarkable, transforming him from a prisoner to the most powerful man in Egypt under Pharaoh.

Administration and Famine

During the seven years of abundance, Joseph implemented a nationwide plan to store surplus grain. His administration was efficient and far-reaching, ensuring that Egypt was well-prepared for the impending famine. When the famine struck, it affected not only Egypt but also surrounding countries, including Canaan, where Joseph's family lived.

Jacob, hearing of the grain in Egypt, sent his sons to buy food. The brothers, unaware of Joseph's position, traveled to Egypt and found themselves standing before their brother, whom they did not recognize. Joseph, however, recognized them and decided to test their character and repentance.

Joseph accused his brothers of being spies and detained them, demanding they bring their youngest brother, Benjamin, as proof of their honesty. The brothers expressed their guilt and remorse for their past actions against Joseph, believing their current troubles were divine retribution. Joseph overheard their conversation and was moved to tears but continued with his plan to test them.

The brothers returned to Canaan and convinced Jacob to allow Benjamin to accompany them back to Egypt. Upon their return, Joseph hosted them at a feast and continued to test their integrity by placing his silver cup in Benjamin's sack and accusing him of theft. Judah's heartfelt plea to take Benjamin's place, to spare their father the grief of losing another son, revealed the transformation in their hearts.

Reconciliation and Revelation

Joseph, deeply moved by Judah's plea, could no longer contain his emotions. He revealed his identity to his brothers, saying, "I am Joseph! Is my father still living?" (Genesis 45:3). The brothers were initially terrified, but Joseph reassured them, explaining that God had orchestrated the events for a greater purpose: "And now, do not be distressed and do not be angry with yourselves for selling me here, because it was to save lives that God sent me ahead of you" (Genesis 45:5).

Joseph's forgiveness and reconciliation with his brothers are profound moments in the narrative. He invited his entire family to live in Egypt, providing them with the best land in Goshen. Jacob, overjoyed at the news that Joseph was alive, traveled to Egypt, where he was reunited with his beloved son. The family settled in Egypt, and Jacob blessed Pharaoh for his kindness.

Legacy and Lasting Impact

Joseph's story, marked by betrayal, suffering, and eventual triumph, is a testament to God's providence and the fulfillment of His purposes. Joseph's rise to power in Egypt not only saved his family from famine but also positioned the Israelites in Egypt, setting the stage for future events in their history.

The themes of forgiveness and reconciliation are central to Joseph's narrative. His ability to forgive his brothers and see God's hand in his suffering exemplifies a profound faith and understanding of divine sovereignty. Joseph's statement to his brothers, "You intended to harm me, but God intended it for good to accomplish what is now being done, the saving of many lives" (Genesis

50:20), encapsulates the essence of his journey and the overarching theme of God's redemptive plan.

Joseph's legacy continued through his sons, Ephraim and Manasseh, who were adopted by Jacob as his own sons and became tribal leaders in Israel. The tribes of Ephraim and Manasseh played significant roles in the history of Israel, with Ephraim becoming a leading tribe in the northern kingdom.

Joseph's Faith and Character

Joseph's life is a powerful example of unwavering faith and integrity in the face of adversity. From his early dreams to his rise to power in Egypt, Joseph consistently demonstrated a deep trust in God's plan. His refusal to succumb to temptation and his resilience in the face of false accusations and imprisonment reveal a character refined by faith.

Throughout his trials, Joseph's faith never wavered. He recognized God's presence and guidance in every situation, whether in Potiphar's house, in prison, or in Pharaoh's court. His ability to interpret dreams and his wisdom in administering Egypt's resources were seen as divine gifts, further affirming his reliance on God.

Joseph's character also shines through in his interactions with others. His compassion for his fellow prisoners, his fairness in dealing with the Egyptian people during the famine, and his forgiveness of his brothers all reflect a heart transformed by God's grace. Joseph's leadership was marked by humility, wisdom, and a desire to serve others, qualities that endeared him to both Egyptians and his own family.

Theological Significance

The story of Joseph and his brothers carries deep theological significance, highlighting key aspects of God's character and His redemptive plan. One of the central themes is divine providence. Joseph's

journey from betrayal to power demonstrates how God can use even the most painful and unjust circumstances to bring about His purposes. This theme is encapsulated in Joseph's declaration to his brothers in Genesis 50:20, emphasizing that God's intentions are always for good, even when human actions are meant for harm.

Another significant theme is forgiveness and reconciliation. Joseph's ability to forgive his brothers and see God's hand in his suffering serves as a powerful example of grace and redemption. This theme points to the ultimate reconciliation brought about through Jesus Christ, who, like Joseph, suffered unjustly but brought about the salvation of many.

Joseph's story also highlights the theme of God's faithfulness. Despite the many challenges and setbacks Joseph faced, God's promises to Abraham, Isaac, and Jacob continued to unfold. Joseph's life is a testament to the faithfulness of God, who remains true to His word and works all things for the good of those who love Him.

Joseph and Christ: Typology

Many theologians and scholars see Joseph as a typological figure of Christ, drawing parallels between Joseph's life and the life and work of Jesus. Both Joseph and Jesus were beloved sons who were rejected and betrayed by their own people. Joseph's suffering and eventual exaltation mirror the suffering, death, and resurrection of Christ.

Joseph's role as a savior during the famine foreshadows Christ's role as the Savior of the world. Just as Joseph provided physical sustenance to the people of Egypt and his family, Jesus provides spiritual sustenance and salvation to all who come to Him. Joseph's forgiveness of his brothers and his role in reconciling his family also point to Christ's work of reconciliation, bringing humanity back into a right relationship with God.

Joseph's Impact on Future Generations

Joseph's impact extended far beyond his own lifetime. His actions not only saved his family from famine but also positioned the Israelites in Egypt, where they would grow into a great nation. This setting laid the groundwork for the Exodus, one of the most significant events in Israel's history.

Joseph's legacy continued through his sons, Ephraim and Manasseh, who became significant tribal leaders in Israel. The blessings Jacob pronounced over them before his death highlighted their future roles and the lasting impact of Joseph's life. Ephraim, in particular, became a leading tribe, often representing the northern kingdom of Israel in later biblical narratives.

Joseph's story also provided future generations with a powerful example of faith and integrity. His life served as a reminder of God's faithfulness and the importance of trusting in His plans, even when circumstances seem dire. Joseph's legacy of forgiveness, resilience, and faithfulness continued to inspire and instruct the people of Israel throughout their history.

Conclusion

The story of Joseph and his brothers is a profound narrative that illustrates the complexities of human relationships and the overarching theme of God's redemptive plan. From betrayal and suffering to forgiveness and reconciliation, Joseph's journey is a testament to God's providence and faithfulness.

Joseph's ability to see God's hand in his suffering and his willingness to forgive his brothers serve as powerful examples of grace and redemption. His rise to power in Egypt not only saved his family from famine but also positioned the Israelites for their future as a great nation.

The theological significance of Joseph's story, including themes of divine providence, forgiveness, and faithfulness, continues to resonate with readers today. Joseph's life points to the ultimate fulfillment of God's promises in Jesus Christ, who, like Joseph, suffered unjustly but brought about the salvation of many.

Joseph's legacy, carried on through his sons Ephraim and Manasseh, and his impact on future generations, underscores the enduring importance of his story in the biblical narrative. Through Joseph's life, we see a powerful demonstration of God's ability to work all things for good, accomplishing His purposes and bringing about the saving of many lives.

In reflecting on Joseph's journey, we are reminded of the profound truth encapsulated in Genesis 50:20: "You intended to harm me, but God intended it for good to accomplish what is now being done, the saving of many lives." This verse captures the essence of Joseph's story and the enduring message of God's redemptive plan, calling us to trust in His sovereignty and faithfulness, even in the midst of life's greatest challenges.

Chapter 6: The Exodus

Summary: The deliverance of the Israelites from Egypt and their journey through the wilderness.

Bible Verse: Exodus 12:41 - "At the end of the 430 years, to the very day, all the LORD's divisions left Egypt."

The Exodus is one of the most pivotal events in the biblical narrative and the history of the Israelites. It marks the transition from slavery to freedom, from oppression to deliverance, and from disunity to nationhood. The journey of the Israelites from Egypt, through the wilderness, and towards the Promised Land is rich with lessons of faith, obedience, and the unwavering faithfulness of God. This chapter explores the deliverance of the Israelites, their trials and triumphs in the wilderness, and the enduring significance of the Exodus.

The Context of Oppression

For 430 years, the descendants of Jacob lived in Egypt. What began as a sanctuary during the time of Joseph gradually transformed into an era of severe oppression. A new Pharaoh, who did not know Joseph, rose to power and feared the growing population of Israelites. To curb their numbers and prevent any potential threat, he enslaved them and subjected them to brutal labor.

The Israelites' lives were marked by relentless toil and suffering. They built store cities for Pharaoh, worked in the fields, and endured harsh treatment. Despite their suffering, the Israelites continued to multiply, prompting Pharaoh to take even more drastic measures. He ordered the midwives to kill all newborn Hebrew boys. However, the midwives, fearing God, defied Pharaoh's orders and allowed the boys to live.

One of these boys was Moses, whose mother hid him for three months. When she could no longer keep him hidden, she placed him in a basket and set it among the reeds along the bank of the Nile. Pharaoh's daughter discovered the basket and, moved by compassion, decided to raise the child as her own.

Thus, Moses grew up in the Egyptian palace, receiving the best education and training.

Moses' Call and Commission

Despite his privileged upbringing, Moses never forgot his Hebrew roots. One day, seeing an Egyptian beating a Hebrew, Moses intervened and killed the Egyptian. Fearing for his life, he fled to the land of Midian, where he started a new life as a shepherd. It was here, in the wilderness, that God called Moses to lead His people out of Egypt.

While tending his father-in-law Jethro's flock, Moses encountered a burning bush that was not consumed by the fire. Intrigued, he approached the bush, and God spoke to him, saying, "I have indeed seen the misery of my people in Egypt. I have heard them crying out because of their slave drivers, and I am concerned about their suffering. So I have come down to rescue them from the hand of the Egyptians and to bring them up out of that land into a good and spacious land, a land flowing with milk and honey" (Exodus 3:7-8).

God commissioned Moses to return to Egypt and confront Pharaoh, demanding the release of the Israelites. Despite his initial reluctance and feelings of inadequacy, Moses obeyed God's call. God reassured him, promising that He would be with him and provide signs and wonders to validate his mission.

The Plagues and Pharaoh's Resistance

Moses returned to Egypt, accompanied by his brother Aaron, who would serve as his spokesperson. They confronted Pharaoh with God's demand: "Let my people go, so that they may hold a festival to me in the wilderness" (Exodus 5:1). Pharaoh's heart was hardened, and he refused, intensifying the Israelites' labor instead.

In response, God unleashed a series of ten plagues upon Egypt, each demonstrating His power and sovereignty. The plagues struck at the heart of Egyptian life and religion, challenging their gods and disrupting their daily existence. The plagues included:

1. The Plague of Blood: The Nile River turned to blood, killing fish and making the water undrinkable.

2. The Plague of Frogs: Frogs swarmed the land, entering houses and disrupting daily life.

3. The Plague of Gnats: Gnats infested the land, covering people and animals.

4. The Plague of Flies: Swarms of flies filled Egyptian homes and land, causing great distress.

5. The Plague of Livestock: A severe pestilence killed the Egyptians' livestock.

6. The Plague of Boils: Painful boils broke out on Egyptians and their animals.

7. The Plague of Hail: A devastating hailstorm destroyed crops and livestock in the fields.

8. The Plague of Locusts: Locusts consumed all remaining vegetation.

9. The Plague of Darkness: Darkness covered Egypt for three days, a tangible sign of God's power over their sun god, Ra.

10. The Plague on the Firstborn: The final and most devastating plague was the death of all firstborn in Egypt, both human and animal.

The final plague broke Pharaoh's resistance. He summoned Moses and Aaron during the night and urged them to leave Egypt immediately. The Israelites, who had prepared for this moment by following God's instructions to sacrifice a lamb and mark their doorposts with its blood, were spared from the plague of the firstborn. This event, known as Passover, became a lasting memorial of God's deliverance.

The Departure from Egypt

The Israelites left Egypt in haste, carrying with them their unleavened bread, belongings, and the wealth of the Egyptians, who gave them gold, silver, and clothing. This departure marked the beginning of their journey to freedom, a journey that would test their faith and obedience.

God led the Israelites through the wilderness by a pillar of cloud by day and a pillar of fire by night, guiding and protecting them. However, Pharaoh's heart hardened once more, and he pursued the Israelites with his army, trapping them by the Red Sea. In their fear, the Israelites cried out to God, and Moses reassured them, saying, "Do not be afraid. Stand firm and you will see the deliverance the LORD will bring you today. The Egyptians you see today you will never see again. The LORD will fight for you; you need only to be still" (Exodus 14:13-14).

God commanded Moses to stretch out his staff over the sea, and He divided the waters, allowing the Israelites to cross on dry ground. As the Egyptians pursued, God caused the waters to return, drowning Pharaoh's army. This miraculous deliverance was a powerful demonstration of God's sovereignty and His commitment to His people.

Journey Through the Wilderness

The journey through the wilderness was marked by both divine provision and human rebellion. Despite witnessing God's mighty acts, the Israelites often struggled with doubt and disobedience. Their journey from the Red Sea to Mount Sinai and beyond was a time of testing and growth, as God shaped them into a covenant community.

Provision of Manna and Quail

One of the first challenges the Israelites faced in the wilderness was a lack of food and water. They grumbled against Moses and Aaron, longing for the food they had in Egypt. In response, God provided manna, a bread-like substance that appeared each morning, and quail in the evening. God instructed the Israelites to gather only what they needed for each day, testing their obedience and trust in His provision.

The provision of manna was a daily reminder of God's faithfulness and care. It also taught the Israelites to rely on Him for their sustenance and to follow His instructions. Despite this miraculous provision, the Israelites continued to grumble and test God's patience.

Water from the Rock

At Rephidim, the Israelites faced another crisis when they found no water. They quarreled with Moses, accusing him of bringing them out of Egypt to die of thirst. In response, God instructed Moses to strike a rock at Horeb with his staff, and water gushed out, providing for the people's needs. This event highlighted both God's provision and the people's persistent lack of faith.

The Battle with Amalek

As the Israelites journeyed, they encountered the Amalekites, a hostile tribe that attacked them at Rephidim. Moses commanded Joshua to lead the Israelites in battle while he stood on a hill with the staff of God in his hand. As long as Moses held up his hands, the Israelites prevailed, but when he lowered them, the Amalekites gained the advantage. Aaron and Hur supported Moses' hands, ensuring the Israelites' victory. This battle demonstrated the importance of faith, leadership, and community support in overcoming challenges.

Covenant at Mount Sinai

The journey led the Israelites to Mount Sinai, where God established His covenant with them. This covenant was foundational to their identity as a people and their relationship with God. At Sinai, God revealed His law, which would guide their worship, conduct, and community life.

The Ten Commandments

God's revelation at Sinai began with the Ten Commandments, delivered in the midst of thunder, lightning, and a thick cloud. These commandments outlined fundamental principles for the Israelites' relationship with God and each other. They included:

1. You shall have no other gods before me.
2. You shall not make for yourself an idol.
3. You shall not misuse the name of the LORD your God.
4. Remember the Sabbath day by keeping it holy.
5. Honor your father and your mother.
6. You shall not murder.
7. You shall not commit adultery.
8. You shall not steal.
9. You shall not give false testimony against your neighbor.

10. You shall not covet.

These commandments formed the basis of the covenant, emphasizing the Israelites' exclusive devotion to God and ethical behavior towards one another.

The Book of the Covenant

In addition to the Ten Commandments, God provided further laws and regulations, known as the Book of the Covenant. These laws addressed various aspects of Israelite life, including social justice, property rights, and religious practices. They were designed to create a just and holy community, reflecting God's character and values.

The Golden Calf and Covenant Renewal

While Moses was on the mountain receiving the law, the Israelites grew impatient and demanded that Aaron make them a god to lead them. Aaron fashioned a golden calf, and the people engaged in idolatrous worship. This act of rebellion provoked God's anger, and He threatened to destroy the Israelites. Moses interceded on their behalf, pleading for God's mercy.

When Moses descended the mountain and saw the idolatry, he shattered the stone tablets in anger. He confronted Aaron and the people, and those who remained faithful to God executed the instigators of the rebellion. Moses then returned to the mountain to plead for God's forgiveness and to receive new tablets.

God graciously renewed the covenant, reaffirming His promises and reissuing the law. This renewal emphasized both God's mercy and the seriousness of the Israelites' commitment to the covenant.

The Tabernacle and God's Presence

As part of the covenant, God provided detailed instructions for the construction of the Tabernacle, a portable sanctuary where He would dwell among His people. The Tabernacle represented God's presence and served as the center of Israelite worship.

The construction of the Tabernacle involved the entire community, with each person contributing materials and labor. Skilled artisans, inspired by God's

Spirit, crafted the intricate furnishings and decorations. The completed Tabernacle was a tangible expression of the Israelites' devotion and a visible reminder of God's presence.

The Tabernacle's layout and furnishings symbolized various aspects of the Israelites' relationship with God. The outer court, the Holy Place, and the Most Holy Place (or Holy of Holies) represented increasing levels of holiness and access to God's presence. The Ark of the Covenant, placed in the Holy of Holies, contained the stone tablets of the law and symbolized God's covenant with His people.

The Journey to the Promised Land

With the Tabernacle completed, the Israelites continued their journey towards the Promised Land. This journey was marked by further challenges, rebellion, and divine intervention.

Spies and the Rebellion at Kadesh

As the Israelites approached the southern border of Canaan, Moses sent twelve spies to explore the land. After forty days, the spies returned with a mixed report. They confirmed the land's fertility but expressed fear about the formidable inhabitants and fortified cities.

Ten of the spies discouraged the people, leading to widespread panic and rebellion. They wanted to return to Egypt, doubting God's promise and power. Only Caleb and Joshua, two of the spies, encouraged the people to trust in God and take possession of the land.

In response to the rebellion, God declared that the current generation, except for Caleb and Joshua, would not enter the Promised Land. The Israelites were sentenced to wander in the wilderness for forty years, until the faithless generation had passed away.

Korah's Rebellion

During the wilderness journey, there were further instances of rebellion, including Korah's challenge to Moses' and Aaron's leadership. Korah, along with Dathan, Abiram, and 250 prominent leaders, accused Moses and Aaron of exalting themselves above the community. They demanded a share in the priesthood.

God intervened dramatically to affirm His chosen leaders. The ground opened up and swallowed Korah and his followers, while fire consumed the 250 men offering incense. This event reinforced the seriousness of rebellion against God's appointed leaders and the sanctity of the priesthood.

The Bronze Serpent

As the Israelites continued their journey, they faced ongoing challenges, including lack of water, difficult terrain, and encounters with hostile nations. Their persistent grumbling and lack of faith provoked God's anger.

At one point, the Israelites spoke against God and Moses, leading to a plague of venomous snakes. Many people were bitten and died. In response to their repentance, God instructed Moses to make a bronze serpent and set it on a pole. Anyone who looked at the bronze serpent would be healed.

This event foreshadowed the ultimate act of salvation through Jesus Christ, who likened Himself to the bronze serpent in John 3:14-15: "Just as Moses lifted up the snake in the wilderness, so the Son of Man must be lifted up, that everyone who believes may have eternal life in him."

Preparations for Entering the Promised Land

As the forty years of wandering drew to a close, the Israelites approached the Promised Land once more. Moses, now an old man, prepared the people for the transition in leadership and the challenges ahead.

Moses' Farewell and the Transfer of Leadership

Moses delivered a series of farewell speeches, recapitulating the law and urging the Israelites to remain faithful to God. These speeches, recorded in the book of Deuteronomy, emphasized the importance of obedience, loyalty, and trust in God's promises.

Moses also commissioned Joshua as his successor, publicly affirming his leadership. He encouraged Joshua to be strong and courageous, assuring him of God's presence and guidance. Moses' final act was to ascend Mount Nebo, where he viewed the Promised Land before his death.

Crossing the Jordan River

Under Joshua's leadership, the Israelites prepared to cross the Jordan River and enter the Promised Land. God instructed Joshua to have the priests carry the Ark of the Covenant into the river. As the priests' feet touched the water, the river stopped flowing, allowing the people to cross on dry ground.

This miraculous crossing paralleled the crossing of the Red Sea, reinforcing God's power and faithfulness. The Israelites set up twelve stones as a memorial to this event, reminding future generations of God's deliverance.

Conquest and Settlement of Canaan

The conquest of Canaan was a challenging and prolonged process, marked by both victories and setbacks. The Israelites faced formidable enemies and fortified cities, but God's guidance and intervention ensured their success.

The Fall of Jericho

The first major conquest was the city of Jericho, known for its strong walls. God provided specific instructions for the Israelites to march around the city for seven days, with the priests blowing trumpets and the Ark of the Covenant leading the way. On the seventh day, the walls of Jericho collapsed, allowing the Israelites to take the city.

The fall of Jericho demonstrated the power of faith and obedience. It also served as a warning to the other Canaanite cities of the Israelites' divine mandate and the consequences of resisting God's plan.

Challenges and Victories

Despite the initial success, the Israelites faced challenges, including internal disobedience and external opposition. At Ai, a smaller city, the Israelites initially suffered defeat due to Achan's sin of taking forbidden items from Jericho. After dealing with the sin and seeking God's guidance, they regrouped and successfully captured Ai.

The conquest continued with a series of battles and alliances. The Israelites' victories were attributed to God's guidance and their unity under Joshua's leadership. Key victories included the defeat of the Amorite kings, the southern and northern campaigns, and the capture of key cities like Hebron and Hazor.

Division of the Land

After the major conquests, Joshua led the division of the land among the twelve tribes of Israel. This process was carried out by lot, ensuring a fair and divinely guided distribution. Each tribe received a specific territory, fulfilling God's promise to Abraham, Isaac, and Jacob.

The division of the land was not only a practical necessity but also a symbolic act of God's faithfulness. It established the tribes in their inheritance and provided a foundation for their future growth and development as a nation.

Covenant Renewal at Shechem

As Joshua's leadership neared its end, he gathered the Israelites at Shechem for a covenant renewal ceremony. This event reinforced the centrality of the covenant and the importance of faithfulness to God.

Joshua recounted the history of God's dealings with Israel, from the call of Abraham to the present. He challenged the people to choose whom they would serve, declaring his own commitment: "But as for me and my household, we will serve the LORD" (Joshua 24:15).

The people reaffirmed their allegiance to God, renewing their commitment to the covenant. This ceremony served as a reminder of their identity as God's chosen people and their responsibility to uphold His commands.

Enduring Significance of the Exodus

The Exodus is a foundational event in the history of Israel and the broader biblical narrative. It established the Israelites as a distinct nation, bound by a covenant relationship with God. The themes of deliverance, faith, obedience, and divine faithfulness resonate throughout the Scriptures.

The Exodus also foreshadows the ultimate act of deliverance through Jesus Christ. Just as God delivered the Israelites from slavery in Egypt, Christ delivers humanity from the bondage of sin. The Passover, commemorating the Israelites' deliverance, finds its fulfillment in the sacrificial death of Christ, the Lamb of God.

The journey through the wilderness, with its trials and triumphs, mirrors the Christian life. Believers are called to trust in God's provision, follow His guidance, and remain faithful despite challenges. The Tabernacle, representing God's presence, points to the indwelling of the Holy Spirit in believers, guiding and empowering them in their journey.

Conclusion

The Exodus is a powerful testament to God's sovereignty, faithfulness, and redemptive plan. From the oppression in Egypt to the crossing of the Jordan River, the journey of the Israelites is marked by divine intervention, testing, and growth. The themes of deliverance, covenant, and faithfulness continue to inspire and instruct believers today.

The story of the Exodus calls us to remember God's mighty acts, trust in His promises, and live in faithful obedience to His commands. It reminds us that God is with us in our journey, guiding, providing, and shaping us into His covenant community. Through the Exodus, we see a glimpse of God's ultimate plan of redemption, fulfilled in Jesus Christ, the Savior of the world.

Bible Verse: Exodus 12:41 - "At the end of the 430 years, to the very day, all the LORD's divisions left Egypt." This verse encapsulates the fulfillment of God's promise and the beginning of a new chapter in the history of His people, a chapter marked by deliverance, covenant, and the journey towards the Promised Land.

Chapter 7: The Giving of the Law

Summary: The receiving of the Ten Commandments at Mount Sinai and the establishment of the covenant.

Bible Verse: Exodus 20:1-2 - "And God spoke all these words: 'I am the LORD your God, who brought you out of Egypt, out of the land of slavery.'"

The giving of the Law at Mount Sinai marks a defining moment in the history of the Israelites and their relationship with God. This event not only provided the foundation for their legal and moral code but also established a covenant that would shape their identity and destiny as God's chosen people. This chapter delves into the significance of the Ten Commandments, the broader context of the covenant, and the implications for the Israelites and future generations.

Arrival at Mount Sinai

After the dramatic escape from Egypt and the miraculous crossing of the Red Sea, the Israelites journeyed through the wilderness, facing numerous challenges and divine interventions. Their arrival at Mount Sinai, approximately three months after leaving Egypt, was a pivotal moment. It was here that God would formally establish His covenant with the people He had redeemed.

Mount Sinai, also known as Horeb, was a place of divine encounter. The mountain itself became a symbol of God's presence and holiness. As the Israelites camped at the foot of the mountain, Moses ascended to meet with God. It was during these encounters that God laid out His intentions and instructions for His people.

The Covenant Proposal

God's initial communication with Moses included a proposal for a covenant. In Exodus 19:3-6, God outlined the terms of the covenant and the special relationship He intended to establish with the Israelites:

"Then Moses went up to God, and the LORD called to him from the mountain and said, 'This is what you are to say to the descendants of Jacob and what you are to tell the people of Israel: "You yourselves have seen what I did to Egypt, and how I carried you on eagles' wings and brought you to myself. Now if you obey me fully and keep my covenant, then out of all nations you will be my treasured possession. Although the whole earth is mine, you will be for me a kingdom of priests and a holy nation." These are the words you are to speak to the Israelites.'"

Moses conveyed God's message to the people, and they responded unanimously, "We will do everything the LORD has said" (Exodus 19:8). This commitment set the stage for the formal establishment of the covenant, marked by the giving of the Law.

Preparations for the Divine Encounter

God instructed Moses to consecrate the people in preparation for a divine encounter. This involved washing their clothes and abstaining from certain activities to symbolize their purity and readiness to meet with God. The people were also instructed to maintain a boundary around the mountain, emphasizing the holiness of the event and the reverence required.

On the third day, amidst thunder, lightning, a thick cloud, and the sound of a trumpet, God descended upon Mount Sinai in fire. The entire mountain trembled, and smoke billowed up like from a furnace. The dramatic display of God's power and holiness created an atmosphere of awe and fear among the people.

The Ten Commandments

Amidst this awe-inspiring scene, God spoke directly to the Israelites, delivering the Ten Commandments, which would become the cornerstone of their moral and legal framework. The Ten Commandments are recorded in Exodus 20:1-17 and encompass both duties to God and responsibilities to fellow humans.

Duties to God

1. You shall have no other gods before me. This command emphasizes the exclusivity of the Israelites' worship and loyalty to Yahweh. It rejects the

polytheism prevalent in surrounding cultures and establishes the foundation for monotheistic worship.

2. You shall not make for yourself an idol. This command prohibits the creation and worship of physical representations of God. It underscores the transcendence and uniqueness of Yahweh, who cannot be confined to an image or form.

3. You shall not misuse the name of the LORD your God. This command forbids using God's name in vain, whether through false oaths, frivolous speech, or blasphemy. It highlights the reverence and respect due to God's holy name.

4. Remember the Sabbath day by keeping it holy. This command institutes a weekly day of rest and worship. It reflects God's rest after creation and serves as a sign of the covenant, reminding the Israelites of their relationship with God and their dependence on His provision.

Duties to Fellow Humans

5. Honor your father and your mother. This command emphasizes the importance of familial respect and authority. It underscores the foundational role of the family in the social and spiritual life of the community.

6. You shall not murder. This command prohibits the taking of innocent life, affirming the sanctity of human life created in God's image.

7. You shall not commit adultery. This command upholds the sanctity of marriage and sexual purity, protecting the family unit and fostering trust within the community.

8. You shall not steal. This command forbids taking what belongs to others, promoting respect for property and honesty in dealings.

9. You shall not give false testimony against your neighbor. This command prohibits lying and deceit, particularly in legal contexts. It upholds the value of truth and justice.

10. You shall not covet. This command addresses the inner attitudes of the heart, prohibiting envy and discontent. It calls for contentment and gratitude for God's provision.

The People's Response

The direct revelation of the Ten Commandments left the Israelites in awe and fear. They trembled at the sound of God's voice and the sight of His presence on the mountain. Fearing for their lives, they pleaded with Moses to speak to God on their behalf, promising to listen to him rather than hearing directly from God.

Moses reassured the people, explaining that God had revealed Himself in this manner to instill the fear of the Lord and to keep them from sinning. He then approached the thick darkness where God was, acting as the mediator between God and the people.

The Book of the Covenant

Following the Ten Commandments, God provided additional laws and regulations, known as the Book of the Covenant, recorded in Exodus 21-23. These laws covered various aspects of Israelite life, including social justice, property rights, and religious practices. They were designed to create a just and holy community, reflecting God's character and values.

The laws included provisions for the fair treatment of slaves, protection of property, and restitution for theft and damage. They addressed issues of personal injury, marriage, and family life, as well as guidelines for worship and festivals. The emphasis was on justice, compassion, and respect for the dignity of every person.

Ratification of the Covenant

To formalize the covenant, Moses built an altar at the foot of the mountain and set up twelve stone pillars representing the twelve tribes of Israel. He then sent young Israelite men to offer burnt offerings and sacrifice young bulls as fellowship offerings to the LORD.

Moses took half of the blood from the sacrifices and put it in bowls, and the other half he splashed against the altar. He then read the Book of the Covenant to the people, who responded, "We will do everything the LORD has said; we will obey" (Exodus 24:7). Moses took the blood and sprinkled it on the people, saying, "This is the blood of the covenant that the LORD has made with you in accordance with all these words" (Exodus 24:8).

This ceremony ratified the covenant, symbolizing the binding agreement between God and the Israelites. The blood represented the seriousness and solemnity of the covenant, as well as the commitment of both parties to uphold its terms.

Moses' Ascent and the Giving of the Tablets

After the covenant was ratified, God invited Moses to ascend the mountain again to receive the stone tablets inscribed with the Ten Commandments. Moses, accompanied by Joshua, went up the mountain, while Aaron and Hur remained with the people to handle any disputes.

Moses stayed on the mountain for forty days and forty nights, during which God provided detailed instructions for the construction of the Tabernacle and the establishment of the priesthood. These instructions are recorded in Exodus 25-31 and emphasize the importance of worship and the presence of God among His people.

The Tabernacle, a portable sanctuary, would serve as the focal point of Israelite worship and a visible reminder of God's dwelling among them. The design, materials, and furnishings were specified by God, and skilled artisans, inspired by His Spirit, crafted the intricate elements.

The Golden Calf Incident

While Moses was on the mountain, the Israelites grew impatient and demanded that Aaron make them a god to lead them. Aaron yielded to their demands and fashioned a golden calf from their jewelry. The people proclaimed, "These are your gods, Israel, who brought you up out of Egypt" (Exodus 32:4).

This act of idolatry provoked God's anger, and He threatened to destroy the Israelites. Moses interceded on their behalf, pleading for God's mercy and reminding Him of His promises to Abraham, Isaac, and Jacob. God relented, and Moses descended the mountain with the stone tablets.

When Moses saw the idolatry and revelry, he shattered the tablets in anger. He confronted Aaron and the people, and those who remained faithful to God executed the instigators of the rebellion. Moses then returned to the mountain to plead for God's forgiveness and to receive new tablets.

Renewal of the Covenant

God graciously renewed the covenant, reaffirming His promises and reissuing the law. Moses chiseled out two new stone tablets and ascended the mountain again. God revealed His character to Moses, declaring, "The LORD, the LORD, the compassionate and gracious God, slow to anger, abounding in love and faithfulness, maintaining love to thousands, and forgiving wickedness, rebellion and sin. Yet he does not leave the guilty unpunished; he punishes the children and their children for the sin of the parents to the third and fourth generation" (Exodus 34:6-7).

Moses interceded for the people, and God renewed the covenant, emphasizing the importance of obedience and loyalty. He reiterated key commandments and provided further instructions for worship and community life.

The Significance of the Law

The giving of the Law at Mount Sinai was a foundational event that shaped the identity and destiny of the Israelites. The Ten Commandments and the broader legal code provided a framework for their relationship with God and each other. The Law emphasized the holiness of God and the need for the Israelites to reflect His character in their conduct.

The Law served several key purposes:

1. Revelation of God's Character: The Law revealed God's holiness, justice, and love. It provided a standard of righteousness that reflected His nature and will.

2. Covenant Relationship: The Law established the terms of the covenant between God and the Israelites. It outlined their responsibilities and the blessings of obedience, as well as the consequences of disobedience.

3. Moral and Ethical Guidance: The Law provided moral and ethical guidelines for the Israelites' conduct. It addressed issues of worship, justice, family life, and community relations, promoting a just and holy society.

4. Preparation for the Messiah: The Law foreshadowed the coming of the Messiah and the new covenant. It highlighted the need for a savior and pointed to Jesus Christ, who would fulfill the Law and establish a new covenant based on grace.

The Enduring Legacy of the Law

The giving of the Law at Mount Sinai had a profound and lasting impact on the Israelites and their descendants. The Ten Commandments and the broader legal code continued to guide their worship, conduct, and community life. The Law also served as a foundation for the teachings of the prophets and the writings of the New Testament.

In the New Testament, Jesus affirmed the importance of the Law and its fulfillment in His life and ministry. He declared, "Do not think that I have come to abolish the Law or the Prophets; I have not come to abolish them but to fulfill them" (Matthew 5:17). Jesus' teachings expanded on the principles of the Law, emphasizing love, mercy, and the transformation of the heart.

The Apostle Paul also addressed the significance of the Law in his letters. He explained that the Law was given to reveal sin and to lead people to Christ. Paul wrote, "Therefore the Law has become our tutor to lead us to Christ, so that we may be justified by faith" (Galatians 3:24, NASB).

The Ten Commandments continue to be a moral and ethical guide for believers today. They reflect timeless principles of worship, justice, and community life that are relevant for all people. The Law also serves as a reminder of God's holiness and the need for a savior, pointing us to Jesus Christ and the new covenant of grace.

Conclusion

The giving of the Law at Mount Sinai is a foundational event in the history of the Israelites and the broader biblical narrative. The Ten Commandments and the broader legal code provided a framework for their relationship with God and each other, emphasizing holiness, justice, and love.

The Law established the terms of the covenant between God and the Israelites, outlining their responsibilities and the blessings of obedience. It also highlighted the need for a savior and pointed to Jesus Christ, who would fulfill the Law and establish a new covenant based on grace.

The significance of the Law endures to this day, providing moral and ethical guidance for believers and reflecting timeless principles of worship, justice, and community life. The Law also serves as a reminder of God's holiness and the need for a savior, pointing us to Jesus Christ and the new covenant of grace.

As we reflect on the giving of the Law at Mount Sinai, we are reminded of the profound truth encapsulated in Exodus 20:1-2: "And God spoke all these words: 'I am the LORD your God, who brought you out of Egypt, out of the land of slavery.'" This declaration affirms God's identity, His deliverance, and His covenant relationship with His people, calling us to trust in His promises and live in faithful obedience to His commands.

Chapter 8: The Spies and the Wilderness

Summary: The exploration of Canaan by the twelve spies and the Israelites' subsequent wandering in the wilderness.

Bible Verse: Numbers 13:27 - "They gave Moses this account: 'We went into the land to which you sent us, and it does flow with milk and honey! Here is its fruit.'"

The journey of the Israelites from Egypt to the Promised Land was marked by divine interventions, acts of faith, and moments of rebellion. Among the most significant events was the exploration of Canaan by twelve spies and the subsequent forty years of wandering in the wilderness. This chapter delves into the exploration, the spies' report, the people's reaction, and the lessons learned from their wilderness experience.

The Command to Explore Canaan

As the Israelites approached the southern border of Canaan, God instructed Moses to send twelve men, one from each tribe, to explore the land. This exploration was not merely a reconnaissance mission; it was a test of faith and obedience. The land of Canaan was the fulfillment of God's promise to Abraham, Isaac, and Jacob—a land flowing with milk and honey, rich in resources and potential.

Moses chose twelve leaders from among the tribes, each respected and trusted within their community. Among them were Caleb from the tribe of Judah and Joshua from the tribe of Ephraim. These men were tasked with gathering information about the land, its inhabitants, the cities, and the fertility of the soil.

The Exploration

The twelve spies set out on their journey, traveling from the wilderness of Paran to various parts of Canaan. For forty days, they traversed the land, observing its cities, fortifications, and agricultural potential. They collected samples of the produce, including a cluster of grapes so large that it had to be carried on a pole between two men. This abundance was a testament to the fertility of the land.

The spies' exploration took them from the Negev in the south to the region around Hebron and as far north as the Valley of Eshcol. They observed the strength and size of the cities, noting the presence of various peoples, including the Anakites, who were known for their formidable stature.

The Report of the Spies

Upon their return, the spies presented their report to Moses, Aaron, and the entire assembly of Israel. Their account began with an affirmation of the land's fertility and abundance. "We went into the land to which you sent us, and it does flow with milk and honey! Here is its fruit" (Numbers 13:27). This confirmation of God's promise should have been a cause for celebration and encouragement.

However, the report quickly turned ominous. Ten of the spies expressed fear and doubt, focusing on the challenges rather than the opportunities. They described the cities as large and fortified, and the inhabitants as powerful. The mention of the Anakites, descendants of the Nephilim, struck fear into the hearts of the Israelites. "We can't attack those people; they are stronger than we are... We seemed like grasshoppers in our own eyes, and we looked the same to them" (Numbers 13:31-33).

In contrast, Caleb and Joshua offered a different perspective. They acknowledged the challenges but emphasized God's power and faithfulness. Caleb urged the people, "We should go up and take possession of the land, for we can certainly do it" (Numbers 13:30). Joshua and Caleb's faith in God's promise stood in stark contrast to the fear and unbelief of the other ten spies.

The People's Reaction

The majority report of the ten spies spread fear and panic among the Israelites. That night, the people wept and grumbled against Moses and Aaron, expressing their desire to return to Egypt. They questioned God's intentions, accusing Him of bringing them to the wilderness to die by the sword. The rebellion reached its peak when they proposed appointing a new leader to take them back to Egypt.

Joshua and Caleb, distressed by the people's response, tore their clothes and pleaded with them not to rebel against the LORD. They reiterated their faith in God's promise, assuring the people that the LORD would be with them and give them victory over their enemies. "If the LORD is pleased with us, he will lead us into that land, a land flowing with milk and honey, and will give it to us" (Numbers 14:8).

Despite their pleas, the assembly was on the verge of stoning Joshua and Caleb when the glory of the LORD appeared at the tent of meeting. God's intervention at this critical moment underscored the seriousness of the people's rebellion and the need for divine judgment.

God's Judgment

God's response to the Israelites' rebellion was swift and severe. He declared that the entire generation of adults who had grumbled and expressed unbelief would not enter the Promised Land. Instead, they would wander in the wilderness for forty years—one year for each day the spies had explored the land—until the last of that generation had died. Only Joshua and Caleb, who had remained faithful, would enter the land.

God's judgment was not only a consequence of the immediate rebellion but also a culmination of the people's persistent disobedience and lack of faith since leaving Egypt. The wilderness journey, which was intended to be a time of preparation and growth, had revealed the deep-seated unbelief and rebellion within the hearts of the Israelites.

Despite this harsh judgment, God did not abandon His people. He continued to provide for their needs, guiding them with the pillar of cloud by day and the pillar of fire by night, and supplying them with manna and water. The forty years of wandering were a time of discipline and instruction, as God sought to shape and refine a new generation that would trust and obey Him.

Lessons from the Wilderness

The forty years of wandering in the wilderness were marked by numerous lessons, both for the Israelites and for future generations. These lessons highlight the importance of faith, obedience, and the consequences of rebellion.

Faith and Obedience

The contrasting responses of the spies illustrate the importance of faith and obedience. Joshua and Caleb's faith in God's promise enabled them to see beyond the immediate challenges and trust in God's power to deliver. Their obedience was rooted in a deep conviction that God would fulfill His word, despite the apparent obstacles.

In contrast, the unbelief of the ten spies and the subsequent rebellion of the people underscore the destructive power of fear and doubt. Their focus on the challenges rather than God's promises led to disobedience and judgment. The lesson is clear: faith in God's promises and obedience to His commands are essential for experiencing His blessings and fulfillment.

The Consequences of Rebellion

The wilderness wanderings serve as a stark reminder of the consequences of rebellion. The entire generation that had witnessed God's mighty acts in Egypt and at the Red Sea was denied entry into the Promised Land because of their persistent unbelief and disobedience. This judgment underscores the seriousness of rebellion against God and the need for repentance and trust.

The deaths of Korah, Dathan, and Abiram, who led a rebellion against Moses and Aaron, further illustrate the consequences of challenging God's appointed leadership. The ground opened up and swallowed them and their followers, serving as a warning to the Israelites of the dangers of defying God's authority.

God's Faithfulness and Provision

Despite the people's rebellion, God remained faithful to His covenant promises. He continued to guide and provide for the Israelites, demonstrating

His patience and mercy. The provision of manna, water from the rock, and protection from enemies were tangible signs of God's ongoing care and commitment to His people.

God's faithfulness is also evident in His discipline. The forty years of wandering were not merely a punishment but a period of instruction and preparation for a new generation. Through these trials, God sought to instill faith and obedience in the hearts of the Israelites, preparing them for the challenges and responsibilities of possessing the Promised Land.

The New Generation

As the forty years of wandering drew to a close, a new generation of Israelites emerged. This generation had grown up in the wilderness, witnessing both the consequences of rebellion and the faithfulness of God. They were poised to enter the Promised Land, led by Joshua, who had proven his faith and leadership.

Moses, now an old man, prepared the people for the transition. He delivered a series of farewell speeches, recorded in the book of Deuteronomy, recapitulating the law and urging the Israelites to remain faithful to God. He emphasized the importance of obedience, loyalty, and trust in God's promises.

Moses also commissioned Joshua as his successor, publicly affirming his leadership. He encouraged Joshua to be strong and courageous, assuring him of God's presence and guidance. Moses' final act was to ascend Mount Nebo, where he viewed the Promised Land before his death.

Crossing the Jordan

Under Joshua's leadership, the Israelites prepared to cross the Jordan River and enter the Promised Land. God instructed Joshua to have the priests carry the Ark of the Covenant into the river. As the priests' feet touched the water, the river stopped flowing, allowing the people to cross on dry ground.

This miraculous crossing paralleled the crossing of the Red Sea, reinforcing God's power and faithfulness. The Israelites set up twelve stones as a memorial to this event, reminding future generations of God's deliverance.

Conquest and Settlement

The conquest of Canaan was a challenging and prolonged process, marked by both victories and setbacks. The Israelites faced formidable enemies and fortified cities, but God's guidance and intervention ensured their success.

The Fall of Jericho

The first major conquest was the city of Jericho, known for its strong walls. God provided specific instructions for the Israelites to march around the city for seven days, with the priests blowing trumpets and the Ark of the Covenant leading the way. On the seventh day, the walls of Jericho collapsed, allowing the Israelites to take the city.

The fall of Jericho demonstrated the power of faith and obedience. It also served as a warning to the other Canaanite cities of the Israelites' divine mandate and the consequences of resisting God's plan.

Challenges and Victories

Despite the initial success, the Israelites faced challenges, including internal disobedience and external opposition. At Ai, a smaller city, the Israelites initially suffered defeat due to Achan's sin of taking forbidden items from Jericho. After dealing with the sin and seeking God's guidance, they regrouped and successfully captured Ai.

The conquest continued with a series of battles and alliances. The Israelites' victories were attributed to God's guidance and their unity under Joshua's leadership. Key victories included the defeat of the Amorite kings, the southern and northern campaigns, and the capture of key cities like Hebron and Hazor.

Division of the Land

After the major conquests, Joshua led the division of the land among the twelve tribes of Israel. This process was carried out by lot, ensuring a fair and divinely guided distribution. Each tribe received a specific territory, fulfilling God's promise to Abraham, Isaac, and Jacob.

The division of the land was not only a practical necessity but also a symbolic act of God's faithfulness. It established the tribes in their inheritance and provided a foundation for their future growth and development as a nation.

Covenant Renewal at Shechem

As Joshua's leadership neared its end, he gathered the Israelites at Shechem for a covenant renewal ceremony. This event reinforced the centrality of the covenant and the importance of faithfulness to God.

Joshua recounted the history of God's dealings with Israel, from the call of Abraham to the present. He challenged the people to choose whom they would serve, declaring his own commitment: "But as for me and my household, we will serve the LORD" (Joshua 24:15).

The people reaffirmed their allegiance to God, renewing their commitment to the covenant. This ceremony served as a reminder of their identity as God's chosen people and their responsibility to uphold His commands.

Enduring Lessons from the Wilderness

The forty years of wandering in the wilderness and the subsequent conquest of Canaan offer enduring lessons for believers today. These lessons highlight the importance of faith, obedience, and reliance on God's promises.

Faith and Trust in God

The contrasting responses of the spies and the people's reaction to their report underscore the importance of faith and trust in God. Joshua and Caleb's faith enabled them to see beyond the immediate challenges and trust in God's power to deliver. Their example calls believers to trust in God's promises, even when circumstances seem daunting.

In contrast, the fear and unbelief of the ten spies and the people led to disobedience and judgment. This serves as a warning of the destructive power of doubt and the importance of cultivating a deep trust in God's faithfulness.

Obedience to God's Commands

The giving of the Law at Mount Sinai and the subsequent instructions for worship and community life emphasize the importance of obedience to God's commands. The Israelites' failure to obey God's instructions resulted in severe consequences, while obedience brought blessings and fulfillment.

For believers today, obedience to God's commands is essential for experiencing His blessings and living a life that honors Him. The Law serves as a guide for moral and ethical conduct, reflecting God's character and will.

The Consequences of Rebellion

The wilderness wanderings and the subsequent events in Canaan highlight the serious consequences of rebellion against God. The entire generation that had witnessed God's mighty acts in Egypt was denied entry into the Promised Land because of their persistent unbelief and disobedience.

This serves as a reminder of the seriousness of rebellion and the need for repentance and trust in God's promises. It calls believers to examine their hearts and align their lives with God's will.

God's Faithfulness and Provision

Despite the people's rebellion, God remained faithful to His covenant promises. He continued to guide and provide for the Israelites, demonstrating His patience and mercy. The provision of manna, water from the rock, and protection from enemies were tangible signs of God's ongoing care and commitment to His people.

God's faithfulness is also evident in His discipline. The forty years of wandering were a time of instruction and preparation for a new generation. Through these trials, God sought to instill faith and obedience in the hearts of the Israelites, preparing them for the challenges and responsibilities of possessing the Promised Land.

Conclusion

The exploration of Canaan by the twelve spies and the subsequent forty years of wandering in the wilderness are pivotal events in the history of the Israelites. These events highlight the importance of faith, obedience, and reliance on God's promises. The lessons learned from the wilderness experience continue to resonate with believers today, calling us to trust in God's faithfulness, obey His commands, and live in alignment with His will.

The story of the spies and the wilderness wanderings serves as a reminder of the consequences of rebellion and the enduring faithfulness of God. It calls us to cultivate a deep trust in God's promises, remain faithful to His commands, and rely on His provision and guidance in our journey of faith.

Bible Verse: Numbers 13:27 - "They gave Moses this account: 'We went into the land to which you sent us, and it does flow with milk and honey! Here is its fruit.'" This verse encapsulates the initial affirmation of God's promise and the potential of the Promised Land, calling us to trust in His faithfulness and rely on His guidance in our journey of faith.

Chapter 9: The Division of the Land

Summary: The conquest of Canaan and the allocation of the land among the Twelve Tribes.

Bible Verse: Joshua 13:7 - "And divide it as an inheritance among the nine tribes and half of the tribe of Manasseh."

The division of the land of Canaan among the twelve tribes of Israel marked the fulfillment of a key part of God's promise to Abraham, Isaac, and Jacob. After years of wandering in the wilderness and intense battles during the conquest, the Israelites were finally poised to settle in their allotted inheritance. This chapter explores the conquest of Canaan, the process of dividing the land among the tribes, and the significance of this division in the broader narrative of Israel's history.

The Conquest of Canaan

The conquest of Canaan was a complex and multifaceted campaign led by Joshua. It began with the miraculous crossing of the Jordan River and the dramatic fall of Jericho, setting the tone for subsequent victories and challenges. The conquest can be broadly divided into several key phases:

The Central Campaign

The initial phase of the conquest focused on central Canaan, establishing a foothold for further operations. The fall of Jericho was a significant psychological and strategic victory, demonstrating God's power and instilling fear among the Canaanite kings. Following Jericho, the Israelites captured the city of Ai after dealing with Achan's sin, which had caused their initial defeat.

The Southern Campaign

The southern campaign was prompted by the alliance of five Amorite kings who sought to resist the Israelite advance. Joshua's surprise night march and the ensuing battle at Gibeon were decisive, with God intervening by sending hailstones and prolonging the day to ensure victory. The Israelites pursued the fleeing armies, capturing key cities and securing control over the southern region.

The Northern Campaign

The northern campaign involved confronting a coalition of Canaanite kings led by Jabin of Hazor. This coalition represented a formidable force, but Joshua's tactical brilliance and God's guidance led to a comprehensive victory. The Israelites captured Hazor and other key cities, breaking the back of Canaanite resistance in the north.

The Process of Division

With the major military campaigns concluded, Joshua turned to the task of dividing the land among the tribes of Israel. This process was carried out under God's guidance and was marked by fairness and adherence to the principles of the covenant. The division of the land can be understood through several key aspects:

The Role of the Lord

The division of the land was not merely a logistical exercise but a deeply spiritual act. It was seen as the fulfillment of God's promise and was carried out in accordance with His will. The use of the lot in determining specific allocations underscored the belief that the Lord was directly involved in the process. Proverbs 16:33 encapsulates this perspective: "The lot is cast into the lap, but its every decision is from the LORD."

The Inheritance of the Tribes

The land was divided among the nine and a half tribes west of the Jordan River, as the tribes of Reuben, Gad, and the half-tribe of Manasseh had already received their inheritance east of the Jordan. The specific allocations were as follows:

1. Judah: The tribe of Judah received a large portion in the south, including the city of Hebron. This region was significant for its association with the patriarchs and its central role in later Israelite history.

2. Ephraim and Manasseh: The descendants of Joseph received substantial territories in central Canaan. Ephraim's inheritance included Shiloh, the site of the Tabernacle, while the half-tribe of Manasseh received land on both sides of the Jordan.

3. Benjamin: Positioned between Judah and Ephraim, Benjamin's territory included Jerusalem, a city that would later become the political and spiritual center of Israel.

4. Simeon: Simeon's inheritance was within the territory of Judah, reflecting the prophecy of Jacob that Simeon would be dispersed among the tribes (Genesis 49:7).

5. Zebulun: Located in the north, Zebulun's territory stretched from the Mediterranean Sea to the Sea of Galilee, encompassing fertile agricultural land.

6. Issachar: Issachar's allotment included the fertile Jezreel Valley, a significant agricultural and strategic area.

7. Asher: Asher's territory was along the Mediterranean coast, providing access to maritime trade and fertile lands.

8. Naphtali: Naphtali's inheritance was in the northern highlands, including the region around the Sea of Galilee.

9. Dan: Initially allocated land in the central coastal region, the tribe of Dan later sought additional territory in the north due to pressure from the Philistines.

The Levitical Cities

The Levites, set apart for religious duties, did not receive a contiguous territory but were given cities scattered throughout Israel. This arrangement ensured that the priests and Levites were integrated into the community, serving as spiritual leaders and teachers. Forty-eight cities, including six cities of refuge, were designated for the Levites.

The Significance of the Division

The division of the land was a fulfillment of God's covenant promises and a critical step in the establishment of Israel as a nation. Several key themes and lessons can be drawn from this event:

Fulfillment of the Promise

The allocation of the land represented the fulfillment of the promise made to Abraham centuries earlier. Genesis 12:7 records God's promise to Abraham: "To your offspring I will give this land." The division of Canaan among the tribes was a tangible manifestation of God's faithfulness to His covenant.

Unity and Diversity

The division of the land highlighted the unity and diversity within the nation of Israel. Each tribe received a specific inheritance, reflecting its unique identity and role within the larger community. Yet, the overall process was guided by a commitment to fairness and adherence to God's will, emphasizing the unity of the people under the covenant.

Responsibility and Stewardship

The inheritance of the land came with responsibilities. The tribes were to steward their territories, adhering to the laws and commands given by God. The land was not merely a possession but a sacred trust, to be managed in accordance with God's principles of justice, mercy, and holiness.

Lessons in Faith and Obedience

The conquest and division of the land also served as lessons in faith and obedience. The victories in battle and the subsequent distribution of the land underscored the importance of trusting in God's promises and following His guidance. The challenges and setbacks, including instances of disobedience, highlighted the consequences of failing to adhere to God's commands.

Challenges and Conflicts

The division of the land was not without its challenges and conflicts. The presence of remaining Canaanite inhabitants, disputes over boundaries, and internal tensions among the tribes presented ongoing issues that required resolution.

The Remaining Canaanites

Despite the successful conquest, many Canaanite cities and regions remained unconquered. The Israelites were instructed to drive out the remaining inhabitants to prevent them from becoming a source of idolatry and corruption. However, in many cases, the Israelites failed to fully obey this command, leading to future conflicts and challenges.

Boundary Disputes

The allocation of the land inevitably led to boundary disputes among the tribes. The need for clear and fair demarcation of territories was essential to maintaining peace and unity. Joshua and the elders played a crucial role in resolving these disputes and ensuring that each tribe received its rightful inheritance.

Internal Tensions

The diversity of the tribes and their distinct identities sometimes led to internal tensions. The case of the altar built by the tribes of Reuben, Gad, and the half-tribe of Manasseh on the east side of the Jordan is an example. This altar was initially misunderstood by the other tribes as a sign of rebellion, but upon investigation, it was revealed to be a memorial of unity and shared worship.

The Role of Joshua

Joshua's leadership was instrumental in the successful conquest and division of the land. His faith, obedience, and commitment to God's commands were crucial in guiding the Israelites through this complex and challenging process.

Faith and Obedience

Joshua's faith in God's promises was unwavering. His confidence in God's guidance enabled him to lead the Israelites with courage and determination. From the crossing of the Jordan to the fall of Jericho and the subsequent campaigns, Joshua's actions were marked by obedience to God's instructions.

Wisdom and Leadership

Joshua's wisdom and leadership were evident in the strategic planning of the military campaigns and the fair distribution of the land. His ability to navigate the complexities of tribal dynamics, resolve disputes, and ensure adherence to God's commands was crucial to the success of the process.

Legacy and Impact

Joshua's legacy extended beyond his lifetime. His final address to the Israelites, recorded in Joshua 23-24, emphasized the importance of faithfulness to the covenant and warned against the dangers of idolatry and disobedience. His leadership set a standard for future generations, and his impact was felt long after his death.

Theological and Spiritual Significance

The division of the land holds deep theological and spiritual significance within the broader narrative of Scripture. It represents the fulfillment of God's promises, the establishment of Israel as a covenant community, and the anticipation of future rest and blessing.

Fulfillment of the Covenant

The allocation of the land was a tangible fulfillment of the covenant promises made to Abraham, Isaac, and Jacob. It demonstrated God's faithfulness to His word and His commitment to His people. The land served as a physical manifestation of the covenant relationship, reinforcing the identity and mission of Israel.

Symbolism of Rest

The division of the land also symbolized rest and fulfillment. After years of wandering and warfare, the Israelites were able to settle in their inherited territories. This rest foreshadowed the ultimate rest and fulfillment promised in the new covenant, realized through Jesus Christ. The book of Hebrews draws a parallel between the rest in Canaan and the spiritual rest available through faith in Christ (Hebrews 4:1-11).

Lessons for Believers

The events surrounding the conquest and division of the land offer enduring lessons for believers today. They call us to trust in God's promises, exercise faith and obedience, and steward the blessings and responsibilities entrusted to us. The unity and diversity within the Israelite community also provide a model for the church, emphasizing the importance of unity in diversity and the shared mission of advancing God's kingdom.

The Legacy of the Twelve Tribes

The division of the land established the foundation for the future development of Israel as a nation. Each tribe's unique inheritance contributed to the collective identity and mission of the people of God. The legacy of the twelve tribes continued to shape Israel's history and spiritual heritage.

The Role of the Tribes

Each tribe played a distinct role within the nation. Judah, with its significant territory and association with Davidic kingship, emerged as a leading tribe. Ephraim and Manasseh, as descendants of Joseph, held influential positions in the northern kingdom. Levi, through its priestly duties, served as the spiritual leaders and mediators between God and the people.

Historical and Prophetic Significance

The history and prophetic literature of the Old Testament frequently reference the twelve tribes. The blessings of Jacob (Genesis 49) and Moses (Deuteronomy 33) highlight the unique characteristics and future destinies of each tribe. The prophets often addressed the tribes, calling them to repentance and faithfulness to the covenant.

The New Testament Perspective

The New Testament continues to affirm the significance of the twelve tribes. Jesus' selection of twelve apostles symbolically represented the restoration and fulfillment of Israel. The book of Revelation envisions the inclusion of the twelve tribes in the eschatological vision of God's redeemed people (Revelation 7:4-8).

Conclusion

The conquest of Canaan and the division of the land among the twelve tribes of Israel marked a pivotal moment in the history of God's people. It represented the fulfillment of God's covenant promises, the establishment of Israel as a nation, and the anticipation of future rest and blessing.

The process of division, guided by God's hand, emphasized the unity and diversity within the Israelite community. It underscored the importance of faith, obedience, and stewardship. The legacy of the twelve tribes continued to shape Israel's history and spiritual heritage, offering enduring lessons for believers today.

The theological and spiritual significance of the division of the land extends beyond the immediate historical context. It points to the faithfulness of God, the fulfillment of His promises, and the ultimate rest and fulfillment found in Jesus Christ. As believers, we are called to trust in God's promises, exercise faith and obedience, and steward the blessings and responsibilities entrusted to us.

Bible Verse: Joshua 13:7 - "And divide it as an inheritance among the nine tribes and half of the tribe of Manasseh." This verse encapsulates the divine directive to allocate the land, symbolizing the fulfillment of God's promise and the establishment of Israel as a covenant community.

Chapter 10: The Judges

Summary: The period of the Judges and the roles they played in leading and delivering the Israelites.

Bible Verse: Judges 2:18 - "Whenever the LORD raised up a judge for them, he was with the judge and saved them out of the hands of their enemies as long as the judge lived."

The period of the Judges is one of the most complex and tumultuous times in the history of Israel. Following the conquest and settlement of Canaan, the Israelites entered a phase characterized by cycles of disobedience, oppression, repentance, and deliverance. This chapter explores the roles of the judges, the challenges faced by the Israelites, and the theological and moral lessons that emerge from this era.

The Context of the Judges

After the death of Joshua, the Israelites found themselves without a central leader to guide them. The conquest of Canaan was incomplete, and many pockets of resistance remained. Moreover, the Israelites struggled to maintain their covenant faithfulness in the midst of Canaanite influence. The book of Judges captures this period of instability and moral decline, where "everyone did what was right in his own eyes" (Judges 21:25).

The role of the judges emerged in this context. These leaders were raised up by God to deliver the Israelites from their enemies and to provide temporary leadership and guidance. The judges were not kings but were charismatic leaders endowed with divine authority and power to fulfill specific tasks. Their stories are marked by both remarkable feats of deliverance and personal flaws, reflecting the complexities of human leadership and divine grace.

The Cycles of Sin and Deliverance

The narrative structure of the book of Judges follows a recurring cycle that highlights the spiritual and moral struggles of the Israelites:

1. Sin: The Israelites fall into idolatry and disobedience, forsaking the covenant with God.

2. Oppression: God allows foreign nations to oppress the Israelites as a consequence of their sin.

3. Repentance: The Israelites cry out to God in their distress, seeking His deliverance.

4. Deliverance: God raises up a judge to deliver the Israelites from their enemies.

5. Peace: A period of peace and stability follows as long as the judge lives.

This cycle repeats throughout the book, demonstrating the Israelites' persistent struggle with faithfulness and the enduring mercy of God.

Key Judges and Their Stories

The book of Judges presents a series of narratives about individual judges, each with unique stories and contributions to Israel's history. Here are some of the most notable judges and their stories:

Othniel

Othniel, the first judge, was a model of faithfulness and divine empowerment. He delivered Israel from the oppression of King Cushan-Rishathaim of Aram. His leadership brought peace to the land for forty years (Judges 3:7-11).

Ehud

Ehud, a left-handed judge from the tribe of Benjamin, delivered Israel from the Moabite king Eglon. His story is marked by cunning and bravery. Ehud assassinated Eglon with a concealed dagger, leading to a successful revolt against the Moabites and eighty years of peace (Judges 3:12-30).

Deborah and Barak

Deborah, a prophetess and judge, stands out as a remarkable leader in a male-dominated society. She provided wisdom and guidance to Israel and, along with the military leader Barak, led a successful campaign against the Canaanite king Jabin and his commander Sisera. The victory was marked by divine intervention, including a thunderstorm that immobilized Sisera's chariots. The song of Deborah and Barak (Judges 5) celebrates this victory and highlights God's sovereignty (Judges 4-5).

Gideon

Gideon's story is one of transformation from fear to faith. Initially hesitant and doubtful, Gideon was called by God to deliver Israel from the Midianites. He famously tested God's call with the fleece and was empowered to lead a small army of 300 men to victory against a vastly larger Midianite force. Despite his initial faithfulness, Gideon's later actions, including the creation of an ephod that became an object of idolatry, reflect the complexities of his leadership (Judges 6-8).

Jephthah

Jephthah, born of a prostitute and rejected by his family, became a valiant warrior and judge. He delivered Israel from the Ammonites but is most remembered for his tragic vow to sacrifice whatever came out of his house to meet him if he won the battle. His daughter was the first to greet him, leading to a heartbreaking fulfillment of his vow (Judges 11-12).

Samson

Samson's story is one of great potential marred by personal flaws. Set apart as a Nazirite from birth, Samson possessed extraordinary strength, which he used to fight against the Philistines. His exploits included slaying a lion, killing a thousand men with a donkey's jawbone, and carrying away the gates of Gaza. However, his weakness for Philistine women, particularly Delilah, led to his downfall. Despite his failures, Samson's final act of pulling down the temple of Dagon, killing himself and many Philistines, demonstrated God's power working through flawed individuals (Judges 13-16).

Theological Themes and Lessons

The period of the Judges is rich with theological themes and lessons that resonate with both ancient and contemporary audiences. These themes include the nature of leadership, the consequences of disobedience, the mercy of God, and the complexity of human character.

The Nature of Leadership

The judges were charismatic leaders raised up by God for specific purposes. Their stories highlight the diverse ways God can use individuals, regardless of their background or personal flaws, to accomplish His purposes. Leadership in the period of the Judges was not about holding a formal office but about being available and responsive to God's call.

The judges' varying backgrounds—from Deborah's prophetic authority to Jephthah's outcast status—demonstrate that God can call and use anyone. This theme encourages readers to recognize that divine calling and empowerment are not limited by human expectations or societal norms.

The Consequences of Disobedience

The recurring cycle of sin, oppression, repentance, and deliverance underscores the serious consequences of disobedience. The Israelites' idolatry and failure to fully obey God's commands led to repeated periods of suffering and oppression. This cycle serves as a stark reminder of the destructive power of sin and the importance of faithfulness to God's covenant.

The narratives also highlight the communal nature of sin and its consequences. The actions of individuals or groups within the community often led to widespread suffering, emphasizing the interconnectedness of the community and the collective responsibility to uphold the covenant.

The Mercy of God

Despite the Israelites' repeated failures, God's mercy and patience are evident throughout the period of the Judges. Each time the Israelites cried out in repentance, God responded by raising up a deliverer. This pattern demonstrates God's unwavering commitment to His people and His readiness to forgive and restore them.

The stories of the judges also illustrate that God's deliverance often comes through unexpected means and individuals. This theme encourages readers to trust in God's providence and to remain hopeful, even in difficult and seemingly hopeless situations.

The Complexity of Human Character

The judges were complex individuals with both strengths and weaknesses. Their stories reflect the multifaceted nature of human character and the reality that even those called by God can struggle with personal flaws and failures. This complexity adds depth to the narratives and provides a more nuanced understanding of divine-human interaction.

The imperfections of the judges serve as a reminder that God works through flawed human beings to achieve His purposes. This theme underscores the importance of humility, repentance, and reliance on God's grace in leadership and service.

The Role of the Spirit

The empowerment of the judges was closely associated with the work of the Spirit of the Lord. The Spirit's presence enabled them to perform extraordinary acts of deliverance and leadership. This divine empowerment is a recurring theme in the narratives and highlights the source of their strength and authority.

The Spirit's Empowerment

The Spirit of the Lord came upon many of the judges, equipping them for their tasks. For example, the Spirit clothed Gideon, enabling him to lead a small force against the Midianites (Judges 6:34). The Spirit's empowerment was a sign of divine favor and presence, ensuring that the judges' actions were aligned with God's purposes.

The Temporary Nature of the Judges' Leadership

The judges' leadership was often temporary and situational, arising in response to specific crises. The Spirit's empowerment was given for particular tasks and did not necessarily translate into long-term authority. This temporary nature reflects the episodic and crisis-driven character of the period and the ongoing need for divine intervention.

Women in the Period of the Judges

The period of the Judges includes notable contributions from women, highlighting their significant roles in the community and God's plan. Deborah and Jael stand out as key figures whose actions had profound impacts on Israel's history.

Deborah

Deborah's leadership as a prophetess and judge is one of the most remarkable aspects of the period. Her wisdom, courage, and faithfulness set her apart as a model of female leadership in a patriarchal society. Her collaboration with Barak and her role in the victory over Sisera demonstrate her strategic and spiritual leadership.

Jael

Jael, the wife of Heber the Kenite, played a pivotal role in the defeat of Sisera. Her decisive action in killing Sisera with a tent peg while he slept in her tent was both daring and significant. Jael's actions are celebrated in Deborah's song and highlight the unexpected ways God can use individuals to achieve His purposes (Judges 4:17-22).

The Transition to Monarchy

The period of the Judges set the stage for the eventual transition to monarchy in Israel. The book of Judges concludes with a sense of instability and moral decline, summarized by the refrain, "In those days there was no king in Israel; everyone did what was right in his own eyes" (Judges 21:25). This refrain reflects the need for a more stable and centralized form of leadership.

The Need for a King

The recurring cycles of sin and deliverance, along with the lack of centralized authority, highlighted the limitations of the judges' leadership. The chaotic and fragmented nature of the period underscored the need for a unifying leader who could provide consistent governance and spiritual direction.

Samuel and the Anointing of Saul

The transition to monarchy began with the prophet Samuel, who played a crucial role in guiding Israel through this significant change. Samuel's leadership bridged the period of the Judges and the establishment of the monarchy. His anointing of Saul as the first king of Israel marked the beginning of a new era (1 Samuel 10).

Theological Reflections on the Judges

The period of the Judges offers rich theological reflections on the nature of God, human leadership, and the dynamics of covenant faithfulness. These reflections are relevant for contemporary readers and provide insights into the challenges and opportunities of faith and leadership.

Divine Sovereignty and Human Agency

The narratives of the judges illustrate the interplay between divine sovereignty and human agency. God raised up the judges and empowered them with His Spirit, yet their actions and decisions also reflected their personal strengths and weaknesses. This interplay highlights the complexity of divine-human interaction and the importance of humility and reliance on God's guidance.

The Role of Memory and Remembrance

The stories of the judges emphasize the importance of memory and remembrance in maintaining covenant faithfulness. The Israelites' repeated forgetfulness of God's acts of deliverance and their subsequent fall into idolatry underscore the need for intentional remembrance. The celebration of victories, such as Deborah's song, served to reinforce the collective memory of God's faithfulness and power.

The Imperfection of Human Leaders

The judges were imperfect individuals, and their stories reflect the reality that human leaders are flawed. This imperfection does not negate their calling or the significance of their contributions but rather highlights the necessity of grace and forgiveness. The narratives encourage readers to recognize the value of imperfect leaders and to seek God's guidance in their leadership.

Lessons for Contemporary Leadership

The period of the Judges offers valuable lessons for contemporary leadership, both within religious communities and broader societal contexts. These lessons emphasize the importance of character, faithfulness, and reliance on divine guidance.

Character and Integrity

The stories of the judges underscore the importance of character and integrity in leadership. Leaders like Deborah and Gideon demonstrated faithfulness, courage, and humility, qualities that are essential for effective leadership. The failures of some judges, such as Samson, also serve as warnings of the consequences of moral compromise and self-indulgence.

Faithfulness and Obedience

The recurring theme of faithfulness and obedience to God's commands is central to the narratives of the judges. Successful leadership was often characterized by a deep commitment to God's will and a willingness to follow His guidance, even in difficult and uncertain circumstances. This lesson calls contemporary leaders to prioritize faithfulness and obedience in their leadership.

Reliance on Divine Guidance

The empowerment of the judges by the Spirit of the Lord highlights the importance of reliance on divine guidance. Effective leadership requires discernment and sensitivity to God's direction. This reliance on divine guidance encourages leaders to seek wisdom and strength beyond their own capabilities.

Conclusion

The period of the Judges is a rich and complex chapter in the history of Israel, marked by cycles of disobedience, oppression, repentance, and deliverance. The stories of the judges highlight the complexities of human leadership, the consequences of disobedience, and the enduring mercy of God.

The judges, as charismatic leaders raised up by God, played crucial roles in delivering the Israelites from their enemies and providing temporary leadership. Their stories reflect the diverse ways God can use individuals to accomplish His purposes, regardless of their background or personal flaws.

The theological themes and lessons from the period of the Judges offer valuable insights into the nature of God, human leadership, and covenant faithfulness. These lessons emphasize the importance of character, faithfulness, reliance on divine guidance, and the recognition of human imperfection.

As we reflect on the period of the Judges, we are reminded of the enduring relevance of these stories for contemporary leadership and faith. The narratives call us to trust in God's promises, exercise faith and obedience, and seek His guidance in our leadership and service.

Bible Verse: Judges 2:18 - "Whenever the LORD raised up a judge for them, he was with the judge and saved them out of the hands of their enemies as long as the judge lived." This verse encapsulates the divine empowerment and guidance of the judges, highlighting God's faithfulness in delivering His people through imperfect human leaders.

Chapter 11: The United Kingdom

Summary: The unification of the tribes under King Saul, and later under King David.

Bible Verse: 1 Samuel 10:24 - "Samuel said to all the people, 'Do you see the man the LORD has chosen? There is no one like him among all the people.'"

The period of the United Kingdom marks a significant era in the history of Israel, characterized by the transition from a loosely connected confederation of tribes to a centralized monarchy. This chapter explores the unification of the tribes under King Saul and later under King David, examining the challenges, achievements, and spiritual implications of this pivotal time.

The Demand for a King

Following the period of the Judges, the Israelites experienced ongoing instability and internal conflicts. The refrain in Judges 21:25 captures the essence of this time: "In those days there was no king in Israel; everyone did what was right in his own eyes." The lack of centralized leadership contributed to moral decline and vulnerability to external threats.

As the last judge and a prophet, Samuel played a crucial role in guiding Israel during this transitional period. Despite his faithful leadership, the Israelites demanded a king to lead them, expressing their desire to be like the surrounding nations. They said to Samuel, "You are old, and your sons do not follow your ways; now appoint a king to lead us, such as all the other nations have" (1 Samuel 8:5).

Samuel was displeased with this request, seeing it as a rejection of God's kingship. However, God instructed Samuel to heed the people's demand, warning them of the implications of monarchy. Samuel conveyed God's message, outlining the potential abuses of royal power, yet the people persisted in their demand for a king.

The Anointing of Saul

God directed Samuel to anoint Saul, a young man from the tribe of Benjamin, as Israel's first king. Saul's physical stature and appearance were impressive, making him an ideal candidate in the eyes of the people. Samuel anointed Saul privately and later presented him to the people at Mizpah, where lots were cast to confirm God's choice.

As Saul was revealed as the chosen king, Samuel declared, "Do you see the man the LORD has chosen? There is no one like him among all the people" (1 Samuel 10:24). The people responded with acclamation, shouting, "Long live the king!" Despite initial reservations, Saul's anointing and acceptance marked the beginning of the united monarchy.

Saul's Reign

Saul's early reign was marked by military successes and efforts to unify the tribes. He led the Israelites in victories against their enemies, including the Ammonites, Philistines, and Amalekites. These victories established Saul's reputation and solidified his position as king.

The Battle Against the Ammonites

One of Saul's first significant challenges came from Nahash the Ammonite, who besieged Jabesh-Gilead. The desperate plea for help from the people of Jabesh-Gilead prompted Saul to rally the Israelites. Inspired by the Spirit of God, Saul mustered an army and achieved a decisive victory, rescuing the besieged city and gaining the people's loyalty (1 Samuel 11).

The Philistine Threat

The Philistines remained a persistent threat throughout Saul's reign. The Philistine garrison at Geba and the subsequent battles at Michmash and other locations highlighted the ongoing struggle. Despite initial successes, Saul's leadership was marred by his failure to fully obey God's commands, particularly in the battle against the Amalekites.

Saul's Downfall

Saul's disobedience and impulsiveness ultimately led to his downfall. His failure to wait for Samuel before offering a sacrifice at Gilgal and his incomplete obedience in the Amalekite campaign were critical moments that revealed his flaws. Samuel rebuked Saul, declaring that God had rejected him as king due to his disobedience (1 Samuel 13:13-14; 1 Samuel 15:22-23).

The Rise of David

God's rejection of Saul set the stage for the rise of David, a young shepherd from Bethlehem. Samuel anointed David privately, recognizing him as God's chosen successor to Saul. David's anointing was marked by the presence of the Spirit of the Lord, signifying divine favor and empowerment (1 Samuel 16:13).

David and Goliath

David's victory over Goliath, the Philistine giant, catapulted him into national prominence. Armed only with a sling and his faith in God, David defeated Goliath, delivering Israel from the Philistine threat and demonstrating his courage and trust in God. This victory endeared David to the people and earned him a place in Saul's court (1 Samuel 17).

David's Service and Persecution

David's service in Saul's court was marked by both favor and tension. He became a skilled musician, a successful military leader, and a close friend of Jonathan, Saul's son. However, Saul's growing jealousy and fear of David's rising popularity led to a series of attempts on David's life. Despite these challenges, David consistently showed loyalty to Saul, refusing to harm the Lord's anointed.

The Civil War and David's Ascension

Saul's relentless pursuit of David forced him into exile, where he gathered a band of loyal followers. During this period, David demonstrated his leadership and strategic acumen, gaining support from various tribes and leaders. Saul's death in battle against the Philistines paved the way for David's ascension to the throne.

David's Kingship in Hebron

Following Saul's death, David was anointed king over the tribe of Judah in Hebron. Meanwhile, Saul's son Ish-Bosheth was declared king over the remaining tribes, leading to a protracted civil war. David's leadership and diplomatic skills gradually won over the northern tribes, culminating in his anointing as king over all Israel (2 Samuel 5:1-3).

David's Reign

David's reign marked a period of consolidation, expansion, and spiritual renewal. He established Jerusalem as the political and spiritual capital, bringing the Ark of the Covenant to the city and uniting the tribes under his leadership.

The Capture of Jerusalem

One of David's first significant acts as king was the capture of Jerusalem from the Jebusites. The strategic and symbolic importance of Jerusalem made it an ideal capital for the united kingdom. David's conquest of the city and its establishment as the City of David signaled a new era of unity and strength (2 Samuel 5:6-10).

The Ark of the Covenant

David's desire to bring the Ark of the Covenant to Jerusalem demonstrated his commitment to making the city the spiritual center of Israel. The joyous procession and celebration surrounding the Ark's arrival highlighted the centrality of worship and God's presence in the life of the nation (2 Samuel 6).

The Davidic Covenant

God's covenant with David, outlined in 2 Samuel 7, is a foundational moment in biblical theology. God promised to establish David's dynasty forever, assuring him that his descendants would rule over Israel. This covenant included the promise of a future Messiah from David's line, a promise that shaped Israel's messianic expectations and is fulfilled in Jesus Christ.

David's Military Campaigns

David's reign was also marked by significant military campaigns that expanded Israel's territory and secured its borders. His victories over the Philistines, Moabites, Edomites, Ammonites, and Arameans established Israel as a dominant regional power.

The Philistines

David's ongoing battles with the Philistines culminated in decisive victories that neutralized their threat. His strategic leadership and military prowess ensured the security of Israel's western border and solidified his reputation as a formidable warrior king.

The Moabites and Edomites

David's campaigns against the Moabites and Edomites further expanded Israel's territory and influence. These victories brought these nations under Israelite control, contributing to the stability and prosperity of David's kingdom.

The Ammonites and Arameans

David's conflict with the Ammonites and their allies, the Arameans, highlighted his ability to form strategic alliances and execute effective military campaigns. The capture of key cities and the subjugation of these nations reinforced Israel's dominance and secured its eastern and northern borders.

David's Administration and Achievements

David's achievements extended beyond military conquests. His administration was marked by effective governance, economic prosperity, and cultural development.

Administrative Reforms

David implemented administrative reforms that strengthened the central government and ensured efficient governance. He appointed capable officials to oversee various aspects of the kingdom, including military, judicial, and religious affairs. These reforms contributed to the stability and effectiveness of David's rule.

Economic Prosperity

David's military victories and strategic alliances brought significant economic benefits to Israel. The expansion of territory and control over trade routes enhanced the kingdom's wealth and resources. David's efforts to develop infrastructure and promote trade further contributed to economic prosperity.

Cultural Development

David's reign also saw significant cultural development, particularly in the areas of music, poetry, and worship. His contributions to the Psalms, as well as his promotion of musical worship in the Tabernacle, left a lasting legacy in Israel's spiritual and cultural life.

Challenges and Failures

Despite his many achievements, David's reign was not without challenges and failures. His personal flaws and the resulting consequences had profound impacts on his family and kingdom.

The Sin with Bathsheba

David's adultery with Bathsheba and the subsequent murder of her husband Uriah were significant moral failures that marred his reign. Nathan the prophet confronted David, leading to his repentance and God's forgiveness. However, the consequences of his sin, including turmoil within his family, were severe and long-lasting (2 Samuel 11-12).

Family Turmoil

David's family was plagued by strife and rebellion. The rape of Tamar by her half-brother Amnon, the subsequent murder of Amnon by Absalom, and Absalom's rebellion against David were tragic events that brought suffering and division. These incidents highlighted the complexities of David's personal life and the far-reaching consequences of sin (2 Samuel 13-18).

The Legacy of David

David's legacy is multifaceted, encompassing his role as a warrior, king, poet, and man after God's own heart. His contributions to Israel's political, military, and spiritual life were profound and enduring.

The Davidic Covenant and Messianic Hope

The Davidic Covenant established an enduring dynasty that became the foundation for Israel's messianic hope. The promise of a future ruler from David's line shaped the expectations of the people and found its ultimate fulfillment in Jesus Christ. The New Testament frequently refers to Jesus as the Son of David, emphasizing the continuity of God's covenant promises (Matthew 1:1; Luke 1:32-33).

The Psalms and Worship

David's contributions to the Psalms and his promotion of musical worship had a lasting impact on Israel's spiritual life. The Psalms, many of which are attributed to David, continue to be a source of inspiration, comfort, and worship for believers. David's emphasis on heartfelt worship and devotion to God set a standard for future generations.

The Model of Leadership

David's leadership, despite its flaws, provided a model of faithfulness, courage, and humility. His willingness to repent and seek God's forgiveness, his dependence on God's guidance, and his commitment to justice and righteousness remain instructive for leaders in all contexts.

Theological Reflections on the United Kingdom

The period of the United Kingdom offers rich theological reflections on themes such as divine sovereignty, covenant faithfulness, leadership, and the anticipation of the Messiah.

Divine Sovereignty and Human Leadership

The narratives of Saul and David highlight the interplay between divine sovereignty and human leadership. God chose and anointed both kings, yet their actions and decisions had significant consequences. This interplay underscores the importance of aligning human leadership with divine purposes and the need for humility and reliance on God's guidance.

Covenant Faithfulness

The establishment of the monarchy and the Davidic Covenant emphasize God's faithfulness to His promises. Despite the people's demands for a king and the failures of their leaders, God remained committed to His covenant. This faithfulness is ultimately fulfilled in the person of Jesus Christ, the true and eternal King.

The Anticipation of the Messiah

The Davidic Covenant and the messianic hope it inspired are central themes in biblical theology. The promise of an eternal ruler from David's line shaped Israel's expectations and provided a framework for understanding Jesus' mission and identity. The New Testament writers frequently draw on this theme, presenting Jesus as the fulfillment of God's promises to David.

Lessons for Contemporary Leadership

The period of the United Kingdom offers valuable lessons for contemporary leadership, particularly in areas such as integrity, humility, reliance on God, and the importance of repentance and forgiveness.

Integrity and Accountability

The stories of Saul and David highlight the importance of integrity and accountability in leadership. Saul's failure to obey God's commands and David's moral failures had significant consequences for their reigns and the nation. These narratives call contemporary leaders to uphold high standards of integrity and to be accountable for their actions.

Humility and Reliance on God

David's life, particularly his willingness to seek God's guidance and his dependence on divine strength, provides a model of humble and reliant leadership. His example encourages leaders to prioritize their relationship with God and to seek His wisdom and strength in their leadership.

The Role of Repentance and Forgiveness

David's response to his sin with Bathsheba, marked by genuine repentance and seeking God's forgiveness, underscores the importance of repentance and restoration. Leaders who acknowledge their failures and seek forgiveness can experience God's grace and continue to fulfill their roles effectively.

Conclusion

The period of the United Kingdom marks a significant era in the history of Israel, characterized by the transition to centralized monarchy and the unification of the tribes under King Saul and later under King David. This period is marked by remarkable achievements, significant challenges, and profound theological themes.

The narratives of Saul and David highlight the complexities of leadership, the importance of covenant faithfulness, and the interplay between divine sovereignty and human agency. The establishment of the Davidic Covenant and the anticipation of the Messiah provide a framework for understanding God's redemptive plan and the fulfillment of His promises in Jesus Christ.

The lessons from this period, particularly in areas such as integrity, humility, reliance on God, and the importance of repentance and forgiveness, remain relevant for contemporary leadership. As we reflect on the United Kingdom, we are reminded of the enduring significance of God's covenant faithfulness and the ultimate fulfillment of His promises in Christ.

Bible Verse: 1 Samuel 10:24 - "Samuel said to all the people, 'Do you see the man the LORD has chosen? There is no one like him among all the people.'" This verse encapsulates the divine choice and anointing of leadership, highlighting the significance of God's guidance and the uniqueness of His chosen leaders in the history of Israel.

Chapter 12: The Reign of Solomon

Summary: The height of Israel's power and glory during the reign of King Solomon.

Bible Verse: 1 Kings 4:20 - "The people of Judah and Israel were as numerous as the sand on the seashore; they ate, they drank and they were happy."

The reign of Solomon marks the zenith of Israel's power, wealth, and international influence. Under Solomon, the kingdom of Israel achieved unprecedented peace and prosperity, becoming a beacon of wisdom and splendor. This chapter explores Solomon's ascension to the throne, his significant achievements, the construction of the Temple, his famed wisdom, and the eventual decline that marred his later years.

Ascension to the Throne

Solomon's path to the throne was marked by political intrigue and divine promise. As the son of King David and Bathsheba, Solomon was not the eldest son, yet he was chosen by David and anointed by God to succeed his father. The transition of power was complex and fraught with challenges.

David's Final Instructions

Before his death, David gave Solomon specific instructions to secure the kingdom and to follow God's laws faithfully. David's charge included dealing with potential threats to Solomon's reign, such as Adonijah, Joab, and Shimei, and establishing his rule firmly based on justice and righteousness (1 Kings 2:1-9).

Solomon's Coronation

Adonijah, another son of David, initially attempted to usurp the throne, but his plans were thwarted by the swift actions of Nathan the prophet and Bathsheba. Solomon was anointed king by Zadok the priest and Nathan the prophet, and he ascended the throne amidst great public support (1 Kings 1:32-40).

Early Reign and Consolidation of Power

Solomon's early reign was marked by decisive actions to consolidate his power and secure the kingdom. His early decisions demonstrated his commitment to justice and the stability of the kingdom.

Execution of Adonijah, Joab, and Shimei

Solomon acted decisively to eliminate threats to his reign. Adonijah, who continued to pose a threat, was executed after he requested to marry Abishag, a move perceived as a challenge to Solomon's authority. Joab, who had supported Adonijah, was also executed, and Shimei, who had cursed David, was placed under house arrest and later executed for violating the terms of his confinement (1 Kings 2:13-46).

Alliance with Egypt

One of Solomon's early political moves was to form an alliance with Egypt by marrying Pharaoh's daughter. This marriage strengthened Israel's international position and secured peace with one of its powerful neighbors (1 Kings 3:1).

Solomon's Wisdom

Solomon's wisdom became legendary, surpassing that of all the known wise men of his time. His wisdom was a divine gift, granted in response to his humble request for discernment in governing the people.

The Dream at Gibeon

Early in his reign, Solomon went to Gibeon to offer sacrifices, and there he had a profound encounter with God. In a dream, God offered to grant Solomon whatever he asked. Solomon's request for wisdom to govern the people pleased God, who granted him unparalleled wisdom, along with wealth and honor (1 Kings 3:5-14).

The Judgment of Solomon

One of the most famous demonstrations of Solomon's wisdom was his judgment in the case of two women who claimed to be the mother of the same baby. Solomon proposed to cut the baby in two, knowing that the true mother would rather give up her child than see it killed. This judgment not only revealed the true mother but also established Solomon's reputation for wisdom and justice (1 Kings 3:16-28).

Building Projects

Solomon's reign was marked by extensive building projects, which showcased the wealth and architectural prowess of Israel. The most significant of these projects was the construction of the Temple in Jerusalem, a central place of worship for the Israelites.

The Construction of the Temple

The construction of the Temple was the fulfillment of David's vision and a central focus of Solomon's reign. Solomon mobilized vast resources, including skilled labor and materials from Tyre, to build the Temple. The construction took seven years and was characterized by meticulous craftsmanship and grandeur (1 Kings 6).

The Temple's design included the Holy of Holies, where the Ark of the Covenant was placed, the Holy Place, and various courts and chambers. The dedication of the Temple was a momentous event, marked by sacrifices, prayers, and the manifestation of God's glory (1 Kings 8).

The Royal Palace and Other Projects

In addition to the Temple, Solomon built a magnificent royal palace, which took thirteen years to complete. He also constructed other significant buildings, including the Hall of Justice, the Palace of the Forest of Lebanon, and fortified cities throughout Israel (1 Kings 7).

Economic Prosperity

Solomon's reign brought economic prosperity and stability to Israel. His administrative and trade policies, along with the peace established through alliances, contributed to this golden age.

Administrative Organization

Solomon reorganized the kingdom into twelve administrative districts, each responsible for providing supplies to the royal court for one month of the year. This system ensured a steady flow of resources and balanced the economic burden across the kingdom (1 Kings 4:7-19).

Trade and Commerce

Solomon established extensive trade networks, leveraging Israel's strategic location. He engaged in trade with neighboring nations, importing luxury goods, gold, silver, and exotic animals. Solomon's fleet of ships, in partnership with Tyre, brought wealth and exotic goods from distant lands, contributing to Israel's prosperity (1 Kings 10:22-29).

International Relations

Solomon's wisdom and wealth attracted the attention of foreign dignitaries, including the famous visit of the Queen of Sheba. His international relations further solidified Israel's standing as a powerful and respected kingdom.

The Visit of the Queen of Sheba

The Queen of Sheba visited Solomon to test his wisdom with hard questions. She was impressed by his knowledge, the splendor of his court, and the prosperity of his kingdom. The visit highlighted Solomon's reputation for wisdom and the extent of his influence (1 Kings 10:1-13).

Alliances and Diplomacy

Solomon's strategic marriages and alliances with surrounding nations ensured peace and stability. His diplomacy and international relations brought wealth and security to Israel, allowing for continued growth and prosperity.

Spiritual Leadership and the Decline

Despite his early achievements, Solomon's later years were marked by spiritual decline and failure to fully adhere to God's commands. His numerous marriages to foreign women led him to idolatry, straying from the exclusive worship of Yahweh.

Idolatry and Compromise

Solomon's marriages to foreign women, who brought their gods and religious practices, led him to build high places for their worship. This compromise displeased God and marked a significant departure from Solomon's earlier faithfulness (1 Kings 11:1-8).

Divine Judgment and Division

As a result of Solomon's idolatry, God declared that the kingdom would be divided after his death. This judgment foreshadowed the eventual split of the united kingdom into the northern kingdom of Israel and the southern kingdom of Judah (1 Kings 11:9-13).

Legacy of Solomon

Solomon's reign left a lasting legacy in various aspects of Israel's history and culture. His contributions to wisdom literature, his building projects, and the international prominence of Israel during his reign had enduring impacts.

Wisdom Literature

Solomon's wisdom is reflected in several biblical books, including Proverbs, Ecclesiastes, and Song of Solomon. These writings encompass a wide range of themes, from practical advice and moral teachings to philosophical reflections on life and love.

The Temple and Worship

The Temple in Jerusalem remained the central place of worship for the Israelites and a symbol of God's presence among His people. Solomon's dedication of the Temple and the associated practices established patterns of worship that continued for centuries.

International Influence

Solomon's reign brought Israel to the height of its political and economic power. The alliances, trade networks, and cultural exchanges established during his reign positioned Israel as a significant player in the ancient Near East.

Theological Reflections on Solomon's Reign

Solomon's reign offers rich theological insights into themes such as divine blessing, human responsibility, wisdom, and the consequences of compromise.

Divine Blessing and Human Responsibility

Solomon's reign began with divine blessing and the fulfillment of God's promises to David. His wisdom, wealth, and achievements were evidence of God's favor. However, Solomon's later failure to uphold God's commands underscores the importance of human responsibility in maintaining covenant faithfulness.

The Pursuit of Wisdom

Solomon's quest for wisdom and his contributions to wisdom literature highlight the value of wisdom in the biblical tradition. Wisdom is portrayed as a divine gift that enables righteous living and effective leadership. Solomon's writings in Proverbs, Ecclesiastes, and Song of Solomon provide timeless insights into the pursuit of a life aligned with God's principles.

The Consequences of Compromise

Solomon's spiritual decline and the subsequent divine judgment illustrate the dangers of compromise and idolatry. His failure to maintain exclusive devotion to Yahweh had far-reaching consequences for his kingdom and legacy. This theme serves as a cautionary lesson on the importance of steadfast faithfulness to God.

Lessons for Contemporary Leadership

The reign of Solomon offers valuable lessons for contemporary leadership, particularly in areas such as wisdom, integrity, humility, and the importance of maintaining spiritual priorities.

The Value of Wisdom

Solomon's reign underscores the value of wisdom in leadership. His ability to govern effectively, make sound judgments, and foster prosperity was rooted in his divinely granted wisdom. Contemporary leaders can learn from Solomon's example to seek wisdom and discernment in their decision-making processes.

Integrity and Accountability

Solomon's later years demonstrate the importance of integrity and accountability in leadership. His moral failures and spiritual compromises had significant consequences. Leaders today can learn from Solomon's example to uphold high standards of integrity and to be accountable for their actions.

Humility and Dependence on God

Solomon's initial humility and dependence on God were key to his early success. His willingness to seek God's guidance and wisdom set a positive example. Contemporary leaders are encouraged to cultivate humility, seek divine guidance, and rely on God's strength in their leadership.

Conclusion

The reign of Solomon represents the pinnacle of Israel's power and glory, characterized by wisdom, wealth, and international influence. Solomon's achievements in building the Temple, his administrative reforms, and his contributions to wisdom literature left a lasting legacy. However, his later years were marked by spiritual decline and compromise, leading to divine judgment and the eventual division of the kingdom.

Solomon's reign offers rich theological insights and valuable lessons for contemporary leadership. The themes of divine blessing, human responsibility, the pursuit of wisdom, and the consequences of compromise remain relevant today. As we reflect on Solomon's reign, we are reminded of the importance of wisdom, integrity, humility, and steadfast faithfulness to God in all aspects of life and leadership.

Bible Verse: 1 Kings 4:20 - "The people of Judah and Israel were as numerous as the sand on the seashore; they ate, they drank and they were happy." This verse encapsulates the prosperity and joy experienced by the people during Solomon's reign, highlighting the period of peace and abundance that characterized his kingdom.

Chapter 13: The Division of the Kingdom

Summary: The split of the kingdom into Israel and Judah after Solomon's reign.

Bible Verse: 1 Kings 12:16 - "When all Israel saw that the king refused to listen to them, they answered the king: 'What share do we have in David, what part in Jesse's son? To your tents, Israel! Look after your own house, David!'"

The division of the United Kingdom of Israel into two separate entities—Israel in the north and Judah in the south—marks a significant and tumultuous period in the history of the Israelites. This chapter delves into the factors leading to the split, the key figures involved, and the immediate consequences of this division. The narrative of the division is rich with political intrigue, prophetic warnings, and the enduring impact of leadership decisions.

The Context Leading to Division

Solomon's reign, though marked by unparalleled prosperity and wisdom, ended on a note of spiritual decline and internal discontent. The seeds of division were sown during Solomon's later years, with his policies and actions contributing to the dissatisfaction among the tribes.

Solomon's Heavy Burdens

Solomon's ambitious building projects, including the Temple and his palace, required substantial resources and labor. To sustain these projects, Solomon imposed heavy taxes and conscripted labor from the Israelites. This burden fell particularly hard on the northern tribes, fostering resentment and unrest.

Religious Compromise

Solomon's marriages to foreign women and the subsequent introduction of idolatrous practices eroded the spiritual integrity of the kingdom. The construction of high places for the worship of foreign gods led to widespread idolatry, compromising the covenantal faithfulness that was central to Israel's identity.

Prophetic Warnings

God, displeased with Solomon's idolatry, raised up adversaries against him, including Hadad the Edomite and Rezon of Damascus. Additionally, the prophet Ahijah delivered a message to Jeroboam, one of Solomon's officials, foretelling the division of the kingdom. Ahijah's prophecy declared that Jeroboam would rule over ten tribes, leaving only Judah and Benjamin under the control of Solomon's lineage (1 Kings 11:29-39).

The Death of Solomon and the Accession of Rehoboam

Upon Solomon's death, his son Rehoboam ascended the throne. Rehoboam's actions in the early days of his reign played a critical role in the unfolding division of the kingdom.

The Assembly at Shechem

Rehoboam went to Shechem for his coronation, where all Israel had gathered to make him king. The people, led by Jeroboam, who had returned from exile in Egypt, approached Rehoboam with a plea to lighten the harsh labor and heavy taxes imposed by Solomon. They promised loyalty in return for a more lenient rule (1 Kings 12:1-5).

Rehoboam's Response

Rehoboam sought counsel on how to respond to the people's request. The elders who had served Solomon advised him to be a servant to the people and grant their request, thereby securing their loyalty. However, Rehoboam rejected their advice and instead followed the counsel of his younger advisors, who recommended that he assert his authority by increasing the burdens on the people (1 Kings 12:6-11).

Rehoboam's harsh response—"My father made your yoke heavy; I will make it even heavier. My father scourged you with whips; I will scourge you with scorpions"—provoked a severe backlash from the northern tribes (1 Kings 12:14).

The Division of the Kingdom

The northern tribes' reaction to Rehoboam's response was swift and decisive. Their declaration of independence from the house of David marked the formal division of the kingdom.

The Revolt of the Northern Tribes

When Rehoboam refused to listen to their pleas, the northern tribes proclaimed their separation from the house of David. "When all Israel saw that the king refused to listen to them, they answered the king: 'What share do we have in David, what part in Jesse's son? To your tents, Israel! Look after your own house, David!'" (1 Kings 12:16). This declaration signaled the end of the united kingdom and the birth of two separate entities: Israel in the north and Judah in the south.

Jeroboam's Kingship

The northern tribes made Jeroboam their king, fulfilling Ahijah's prophecy. Jeroboam established his capital first at Shechem and later at Tirzah. His reign, however, was marked by significant religious and political challenges as he sought to consolidate his rule over the newly formed kingdom of Israel (1 Kings 12:20).

Rehoboam's Attempt to Reunite the Kingdom

Rehoboam initially sought to reunite the kingdom by force. He assembled an army of 180,000 men from Judah and Benjamin to fight against Israel and restore his rule. However, God intervened through the prophet Shemaiah, who delivered a message instructing Rehoboam and the people of Judah not to fight against their fellow Israelites. Obeying the prophetic word, Rehoboam called off the military campaign and returned to Jerusalem (1 Kings 12:21-24).

The Establishment of Religious Centers

One of Jeroboam's significant actions to solidify his rule over Israel was the establishment of alternative religious centers to prevent the people from returning to Jerusalem to worship at the Temple.

The Golden Calves

Fearing that pilgrimages to Jerusalem would weaken his authority, Jeroboam set up golden calves at Bethel and Dan, declaring, "Here are your gods, Israel, who brought you up out of Egypt" (1 Kings 12:28). This act of idolatry was intended to provide a convenient alternative to the Temple in Jerusalem and to reinforce his political control over the northern kingdom.

The Consequences of Idolatry

Jeroboam's establishment of golden calves and alternative religious practices led Israel into sin and idolatry. This departure from covenantal worship had long-lasting spiritual and moral repercussions, setting a pattern of idolatry and apostasy that plagued the northern kingdom throughout its history.

The Early Reigns of Rehoboam and Jeroboam

The early reigns of Rehoboam in Judah and Jeroboam in Israel were marked by efforts to consolidate their respective kingdoms amidst ongoing challenges and conflicts.

Rehoboam in Judah

Rehoboam focused on fortifying his kingdom and securing his rule. He strengthened the defenses of key cities, including Bethlehem, Hebron, and Lachish, to protect against potential invasions from the north and other neighboring nations (2 Chronicles 11:5-12).

Religious Reforms

Rehoboam's reign saw a mix of religious fidelity and apostasy. Initially, he followed the ways of the Lord, and priests and Levites from Israel moved to Judah, seeking to continue their worship according to the Mosaic law. However, as his reign progressed, Rehoboam and the people of Judah fell into idolatry, building high places, sacred stones, and Asherah poles (2 Chronicles 12:1-4).

The Egyptian Invasion

In the fifth year of Rehoboam's reign, King Shishak of Egypt invaded Judah, capturing fortified cities and threatening Jerusalem. Rehoboam and the leaders of Judah humbled themselves before the Lord, and God delivered them from total destruction. However, Judah became a vassal state to Egypt, and the treasures of the Temple and the royal palace were taken (2 Chronicles 12:5-12).

Jeroboam in Israel

Jeroboam's reign was characterized by ongoing efforts to establish his authority and suppress dissent. His establishment of alternative religious practices and centers was central to these efforts, but it also created internal conflicts and furthered Israel's spiritual decline.

Prophetic Confrontations

Jeroboam's actions brought him into direct conflict with the prophets of the Lord. The prophet Ahijah, who had initially prophesied Jeroboam's rise to power, later delivered a message of judgment against Jeroboam's house due to his idolatry. Ahijah foretold the destruction of Jeroboam's dynasty and the eventual exile of Israel (1 Kings 14:7-16).

The Death of Jeroboam's Son

One of the significant personal tragedies in Jeroboam's life was the death of his son Abijah. When Abijah fell ill, Jeroboam sent his wife in disguise to Ahijah to inquire about their son's fate. Ahijah, though blind, recognized her and delivered a message of judgment, declaring that Abijah would die and that Jeroboam's house would be cut off from Israel (1 Kings 14:1-18).

The Long-term Consequences of Division

The division of the kingdom had profound and lasting consequences for both Israel and Judah, shaping their political, religious, and social trajectories.

Political Instability

The northern kingdom of Israel experienced significant political instability, with frequent changes in leadership, coups, and assassinations. Jeroboam's dynasty lasted only two generations before being overthrown, setting a pattern of short-lived dynasties and internal strife that weakened the kingdom.

Religious Apostasy

Jeroboam's establishment of idolatrous worship practices led to widespread apostasy in Israel. Subsequent kings followed his example, perpetuating idolatry and leading the people further away from the covenant with God. This spiritual decline ultimately contributed to Israel's downfall and exile.

Prophetic Warnings and Judgment

Throughout the history of the divided kingdom, prophets played a crucial role in calling the people back to faithfulness and warning of impending judgment. Prophets like Elijah, Elisha, Hosea, and Amos confronted the kings and people of Israel with messages of repentance and divine judgment, highlighting the spiritual and moral consequences of their actions.

The Fall of Israel and Judah

The long-term consequences of division and apostasy culminated in the fall of both kingdoms. In 722 BCE, the Assyrian Empire conquered the northern kingdom of Israel, leading to the exile of its people and the end of its political existence. The southern kingdom of Judah, though lasting longer, eventually fell to the Babylonian Empire in 586 BCE, resulting in the destruction of Jerusalem and the Temple and the exile of its people.

Theological Reflections on the Division

The division of the kingdom offers rich theological insights into themes such as covenant faithfulness, divine judgment, leadership, and the enduring hope of restoration.

Covenant Faithfulness and Divine Judgment

The division of the kingdom underscores the importance of covenant faithfulness and the consequences of apostasy. The idolatry and unfaithfulness of the kings and people led to divine judgment, manifesting in political division, social unrest, and eventual exile. This theme serves as a stark reminder of the seriousness of covenantal obligations and the need for steadfast devotion to God.

The Role of Leadership

The actions and decisions of leaders like Rehoboam and Jeroboam had profound impacts on the fate of their kingdoms. Their failures in leadership—whether through harshness, idolatry, or political maneuvering—highlight the critical role of leaders in guiding their people toward or away from faithfulness to God. This theme emphasizes the importance of wise, just, and godly leadership.

Prophetic Voices and Hope

The prophets' role during the divided kingdom was pivotal in calling the people back to God and providing a voice of hope amidst judgment. Despite the dire warnings and declarations of impending doom, the prophets also spoke of a future restoration and the enduring promise of God's covenant. This dual message of judgment and hope is central to the prophetic tradition and provides a framework for understanding God's redemptive plan.

The Enduring Hope of Restoration

The division and subsequent fall of the kingdoms did not signify the end of God's plan for Israel. The prophetic messages of restoration and the promises of a future Messiah from the line of David pointed to a future hope. This hope is ultimately fulfilled in the person of Jesus Christ, who brings together the divided people and inaugurates a new covenant of grace and truth.

Lessons for Contemporary Leadership

The division of the kingdom offers valuable lessons for contemporary leadership, particularly in areas such as humility, responsiveness to the needs of the people, integrity, and the importance of maintaining spiritual priorities.

Humility and Responsiveness

Rehoboam's failure to listen to the people's grievances and his harsh response highlight the importance of humility and responsiveness in leadership. Leaders today can learn from this example to be attentive to the needs and concerns of those they lead, fostering an environment of mutual respect and cooperation.

Integrity and Accountability

Jeroboam's idolatry and political maneuvering demonstrate the dangers of compromising integrity for political gain. Contemporary leaders are encouraged to uphold high standards of integrity and to be accountable for their actions, recognizing the long-term consequences of their decisions.

Maintaining Spiritual Priorities

The spiritual decline of both Israel and Judah underscores the importance of maintaining spiritual priorities in leadership. Leaders are called to prioritize their relationship with God and to lead with a focus on faithfulness, justice, and righteousness. This focus is essential for fostering a healthy and thriving community.

Conclusion

The division of the kingdom into Israel and Judah marks a significant and tumultuous period in the history of the Israelites. The factors leading to the split, the key figures involved, and the immediate and long-term consequences of this division are rich with lessons in leadership, covenant faithfulness, and the role of prophetic voices.

The theological reflections on the division highlight themes of divine judgment, covenant faithfulness, leadership, and the enduring hope of restoration. These themes remain relevant today, offering valuable insights for contemporary leadership and spiritual life.

As we reflect on the division of the kingdom, we are reminded of the importance of humility, integrity, responsiveness, and maintaining spiritual priorities. The prophetic messages of judgment and hope provide a framework for understanding God's redemptive plan and the ultimate fulfillment of His promises in Christ.

Bible Verse: 1 Kings 12:16 - "When all Israel saw that the king refused to listen to them, they answered the king: 'What share do we have in David, what part in Jesse's son? To your tents, Israel! Look after your own house, David!'" This verse encapsulates the decisive moment of division, highlighting the people's rejection of Rehoboam's harsh rule and the beginning of a new and challenging chapter in Israel's history.

Chapter 14: The Exile

Summary: The fall of Israel and Judah and the exile of the tribes to foreign lands.

Bible Verse: 2 Kings 17:23 - "So the people of Israel were taken from their homeland into exile in Assyria, and they are still there."

The exile of the Israelites marks one of the most significant and traumatic events in the history of ancient Israel. The fall of the northern kingdom of Israel to the Assyrians and the subsequent fall of the southern kingdom of Judah to the Babylonians led to the displacement and dispersion of the tribes. This chapter explores the events leading up to the exile, the experiences of the exiled communities, and the theological and historical implications of this period.

The Context Leading to Exile

The seeds of exile were sown over many generations as the Israelites struggled with faithfulness to their covenant with God. The persistent idolatry, social injustice, and failure to heed prophetic warnings created a context ripe for judgment.

The Northern Kingdom of Israel

The northern kingdom of Israel, established under Jeroboam I after the division of the united monarchy, was plagued by political instability and religious apostasy. Jeroboam's establishment of golden calves at Bethel and Dan set a precedent for idolatry that persisted throughout Israel's history. Subsequent kings followed in his footsteps, leading the nation further away from covenant faithfulness.

Prophetic Warnings

Prophets such as Elijah, Elisha, Amos, and Hosea were sent to call Israel back to faithfulness. Their messages often condemned the idolatry and social injustices of the people and leaders. Despite these warnings, the people largely ignored the prophets' calls to repentance, leading to a gradual but inevitable decline.

The Fall of the Northern Kingdom

The culmination of Israel's unfaithfulness came in the form of conquest and exile by the Assyrian Empire.

Assyrian Ascendancy

The Assyrian Empire, under kings such as Tiglath-Pileser III, Shalmaneser V, and Sargon II, expanded aggressively during the 8th century BCE. Israel, caught in the geopolitical struggles of the region, found itself increasingly vulnerable.

The Siege of Samaria

In 722 BCE, after a prolonged siege, the Assyrians captured Samaria, the capital of Israel. The Assyrian king, Shalmaneser V, and later Sargon II, deported the Israelite population, dispersing them throughout the Assyrian Empire. This policy of deportation aimed to prevent rebellion by scattering conquered peoples and integrating them into the empire (2 Kings 17:5-6).

Theological Interpretation

The biblical narrative attributes Israel's fall to their persistent unfaithfulness to God. 2 Kings 17:7-23 provides a theological explanation, highlighting the people's idolatry, rejection of God's commandments, and disregard for the prophets. "So the people of Israel were taken from their homeland into exile in Assyria, and they are still there" (2 Kings 17:23).

The Southern Kingdom of Judah

The southern kingdom of Judah, though initially more faithful, eventually followed a similar path of decline. The reforms of kings like Hezekiah and Josiah temporarily restored covenant faithfulness, but these efforts were ultimately insufficient to avert disaster.

Hezekiah's Reforms

King Hezekiah (715-687 BCE) enacted significant religious reforms, including the destruction of high places, altars, and idols. His faithfulness was notable, and he sought to centralize worship in Jerusalem. However, Judah's broader societal issues and geopolitical challenges continued to threaten stability.

Josiah's Reforms

King Josiah (640-609 BCE) also sought to restore covenant faithfulness. His discovery of the Book of the Law during temple repairs prompted a national religious revival. Despite these efforts, the reforms could not completely eradicate the deeply entrenched idolatry and social injustices (2 Kings 22-23).

The Fall of Judah

The fall of Judah to the Babylonians occurred over several decades, culminating in the destruction of Jerusalem and the temple.

Babylonian Ascendancy

The Babylonian Empire, under kings such as Nebuchadnezzar II, emerged as a dominant power in the late 7th century BCE. Judah, caught between the declining Assyrian Empire and the rising Babylonians, faced increasing pressure.

The First Siege and Exile

In 597 BCE, Nebuchadnezzar besieged Jerusalem and captured King Jehoiachin. He deported a significant portion of the population, including the elite and skilled craftsmen, to Babylon. This event marked the beginning of the Babylonian exile (2 Kings 24:10-16).

The Destruction of Jerusalem

In 586 BCE, after a rebellion by King Zedekiah, Nebuchadnezzar returned, besieged Jerusalem again, and destroyed the city and the temple. The remaining population was either killed or deported, leaving Judah in ruins (2 Kings 25:1-21).

The Experience of Exile

The exile was a time of profound dislocation and crisis for the Israelites. Removed from their homeland, temple, and traditional worship practices, they faced significant challenges in maintaining their identity and faith.

Life in Exile

The exiled communities in Assyria and Babylon faced the task of adapting to foreign cultures and political systems. While some Israelites integrated into their new environments, others sought to preserve their distinct identity.

Religious Practices

In the absence of the temple, the exiles developed new ways of practicing their faith. Synagogues emerged as centers of worship and community life. The reading and study of Torah became central, helping to preserve religious traditions and teachings.

Theological Reflections on Exile

The experience of exile prompted deep theological reflection and transformation. The exiles grappled with questions of divine justice, covenant faithfulness, and the hope of restoration.

Divine Justice and Judgment

The prophets framed the exile as divine judgment for Israel and Judah's persistent unfaithfulness. Passages like 2 Kings 17:7-23 and Jeremiah 25:8-11 emphasize that the exile was a consequence of their sins. This perspective underscored the seriousness of covenantal obligations and the need for repentance.

Covenant Faithfulness and Identity

The exile challenged the Israelites to reconsider their identity and relationship with God. Despite the judgment, the prophets also conveyed messages of hope and assurance of God's enduring covenantal faithfulness. Passages like Jeremiah 29:10-14 and Ezekiel 36:24-28 promise restoration and renewal.

Hope and Restoration

The prophetic messages of hope and restoration played a crucial role in sustaining the exiled communities. Isaiah 40-55, often referred to as Deutero-Isaiah, contains powerful visions of return and redemption. These passages promise a new exodus, the rebuilding of Jerusalem, and the reestablishment of the covenant community.

Key Figures and Their Contributions

Several key figures played significant roles in shaping the experience and theology of the exilic period.

Jeremiah

The prophet Jeremiah, who lived through the final days of Judah and the early years of exile, provided crucial guidance. His messages warned of impending judgment but also offered hope of restoration. Jeremiah's letter to the exiles in Babylon encouraged them to seek the welfare of their new cities while holding onto the promise of return (Jeremiah 29).

Ezekiel

Ezekiel, a prophet among the exiles in Babylon, delivered vivid and symbolic visions. His prophecies addressed both the reasons for the exile and the hope of restoration. Ezekiel's vision of the valley of dry bones (Ezekiel 37) symbolized the revival of Israel and the renewal of the covenant.

Daniel

The book of Daniel, set during the Babylonian exile, provides insights into the challenges of maintaining faith in a foreign land. Daniel's commitment to his faith, despite pressures to conform, and his visions of God's sovereignty and future deliverance offered hope to the exiled community.

The Return from Exile

The eventual return from exile, prompted by the Persian conquest of Babylon, marked a significant moment of restoration and renewal for the Israelites.

The Decree of Cyrus

In 539 BCE, King Cyrus of Persia conquered Babylon and issued a decree allowing exiled peoples, including the Israelites, to return to their homelands and rebuild their temples. This decree fulfilled prophetic promises and initiated the return of the exiles to Judah (Ezra 1:1-4).

The Rebuilding of the Temple

Led by figures like Zerubbabel and Joshua the high priest, the returning exiles undertook the rebuilding of the temple. Despite opposition and challenges, the foundation was laid, and the temple was eventually completed and dedicated (Ezra 3-6).

The Restoration of Jerusalem

The return also involved the rebuilding of Jerusalem's walls and the reestablishment of the community. Under the leadership of Nehemiah, the walls were rebuilt, and Ezra the scribe led a spiritual renewal centered on the reading and teaching of the Torah (Nehemiah 1-8).

Theological and Historical Significance of the Exile

The exile and subsequent return had profound theological and historical implications for the Israelite community.

Theological Transformation

The experience of exile transformed Israel's theological understanding. The emphasis on monotheism, the centrality of the Torah, and the development of synagogue worship were significant shifts that shaped post-exilic Judaism.

The Formation of Jewish Identity

The exile and return were pivotal in the formation of Jewish identity. The focus on covenant faithfulness, adherence to the Torah, and the hope of messianic restoration became defining elements of Jewish religious life.

The Role of the Prophets

The prophetic literature produced during and after the exile played a crucial role in shaping the theological landscape. The messages of judgment, hope, and restoration provided a

framework for understanding the exile and God's ongoing relationship with His people.

Lessons for Contemporary Faith

The exile offers valuable lessons for contemporary faith communities, particularly in areas such as resilience, hope, and faithfulness.

Resilience in Adversity

The experience of the exiles demonstrates the importance of resilience and adaptability in the face of adversity. The ability to maintain faith and identity despite displacement and challenges is a powerful testimony to the enduring strength of the covenant community.

Hope in God's Promises

The prophetic messages of hope and restoration underscore the importance of holding onto God's promises. Even in the darkest times, the assurance of God's faithfulness and the hope of future restoration provide strength and encouragement.

Faithfulness to Covenant

The exile highlights the significance of covenant faithfulness and the consequences of apostasy. The emphasis on returning to the core principles of the covenant and maintaining a relationship with God is a central theme that continues to resonate.

Conclusion

The exile of Israel and Judah marks a profound and transformative period in the history of the Israelites. The fall of the northern and southern kingdoms, the experience of displacement, and the eventual return from exile are rich with theological and historical significance.

The narratives of the exile emphasize themes of divine judgment, covenant faithfulness, resilience, and hope. The prophetic voices of figures like Jeremiah, Ezekiel, and Daniel provided guidance, warning, and assurance during this challenging period.

The return from exile and the subsequent rebuilding of the temple and Jerusalem marked a new chapter of restoration and renewal. The lessons from the exile continue to offer valuable insights for contemporary faith communities, encouraging resilience, hope, and steadfast faithfulness to God's covenant.

Bible Verse: 2 Kings 17:23 - "So the people of Israel were taken from their homeland into exile in Assyria, and they are still there." This verse encapsulates the reality of the exile, highlighting the displacement and enduring impact of this significant event in Israel's history.

Chapter 15: The Return and Restoration

Summary: The return from exile and the rebuilding of the nation, focusing on the hope and future promises for the tribes.

Bible Verse: Ezra 1:3 - "Any of his people among you may go up to Jerusalem in Judah and build the temple of the LORD, the God of Israel, the God who is in Jerusalem, and may their God be with them."

The return from exile and the subsequent restoration of the nation mark a pivotal and hopeful chapter in the history of Israel. After decades of exile in Babylon, the Israelites were given the opportunity to return to their homeland, rebuild the temple, and reestablish their community. This chapter explores the events leading to the return, the challenges and achievements of the restoration period, and the enduring hope and future promises for the tribes of Israel.

The Decree of Cyrus

The return from exile was initiated by the decree of Cyrus, the king of Persia, who conquered Babylon in 539 BCE. This decree allowed the exiled peoples, including the Israelites, to return to their homelands and rebuild their temples.

Cyrus' Proclamation

In the first year of his reign, Cyrus issued a proclamation that fulfilled the prophetic words spoken by Isaiah and Jeremiah. Ezra 1:1-3 records the decree: "In the first year of Cyrus king of Persia, in order to fulfill the word of the LORD spoken by Jeremiah, the LORD moved the heart of Cyrus king of Persia to make a proclamation throughout his realm and also to put it in writing: 'This is what Cyrus king of Persia says: "The LORD, the God of heaven, has given me all the kingdoms of the earth and he has appointed me to build a temple for him at Jerusalem in Judah. Any of his people among you may go up to Jerusalem in Judah and build the temple of the LORD, the God of Israel, the God who is in Jerusalem, and may their God be with them.'"

This proclamation was a monumental moment for the exiles, offering them the chance to return to their ancestral land and restore their religious and communal life.

The First Return under Zerubbabel

The first wave of returnees was led by Zerubbabel, a descendant of David, and Joshua, the high priest. This group focused on rebuilding the temple and reestablishing worship in Jerusalem.

The Journey Back

The journey from Babylon to Jerusalem was arduous and required significant preparation. The returning exiles carried with them valuable items for the temple, as well as resources provided by Cyrus and the surrounding peoples. The journey itself was an act of faith, as they left behind the relative stability of Babylon for the uncertain prospects of a desolate homeland.

Rebuilding the Altar and Temple

Upon arriving in Jerusalem, the first priority was to rebuild the altar and reinstitute the sacrificial system. Ezra 3:2-3 records this important step: "Then Joshua son of Jozadak and his fellow priests and Zerubbabel son of Shealtiel and his associates began to build the altar of the God of Israel to sacrifice burnt offerings on it, in accordance with what is written in the Law of Moses the man of God. Despite their fear of the peoples around them, they built the altar on its foundation and sacrificed burnt offerings on it to the LORD, both the morning and evening sacrifices."

The rebuilding of the altar was followed by the laying of the foundation of the temple. This event was marked by both joy and weeping, as the older generation remembered the glory of the former temple while the younger generation celebrated the progress being made (Ezra 3:10-13).

Opposition and Challenges

The rebuilding efforts faced significant opposition from the surrounding peoples. These adversaries sought to discourage and intimidate the builders, using political and legal means to halt the construction. Despite these challenges, the prophets Haggai and Zechariah encouraged the people to persevere and continue the work (Ezra 4-5; Haggai 1-2; Zechariah 1-8).

The Ministry of the Prophets Haggai and Zechariah

Haggai and Zechariah played crucial roles in motivating and guiding the returnees during the restoration period. Their messages addressed both the immediate challenges and the future hope for Israel.

Haggai's Encouragement

Haggai's ministry began in the second year of King Darius' reign. His messages emphasized the importance of prioritizing the rebuilding of the temple and reassured the people of God's presence and blessing. Haggai 2:4-5 conveys this encouragement: "But now be strong, Zerubbabel,' declares the LORD. 'Be strong, Joshua son of Jozadak, the high priest. Be strong, all you people of the land,' declares the LORD, 'and work. For I am with you,' declares the LORD Almighty. 'This is what I covenanted with you when you came out of Egypt. And my Spirit remains among you. Do not fear.'"

Zechariah's Visions

Zechariah's prophecies included a series of visions that provided both immediate and eschatological hope. His messages emphasized God's sovereignty, the coming of the Messiah, and the ultimate restoration of Israel. Zechariah 8:3 captures this promise: "This is what the LORD says: 'I will return to Zion and dwell in Jerusalem. Then Jerusalem will be called the Faithful City, and the mountain of the LORD Almighty will be called the Holy Mountain.'"

The Completion of the Temple

Despite the opposition and delays, the temple was eventually completed in the sixth year of King Darius' reign. The dedication of the temple was a significant event, marked by sacrifices, celebrations, and the observance of the Passover.

The Dedication Ceremony

Ezra 6:15-16 describes the completion and dedication of the temple: "The temple was completed on the third day of the month Adar, in the sixth year of the reign of King Darius. Then the people of Israel—the priests, the Levites and the rest of the exiles—celebrated the dedication of the house of God with joy." This dedication reaffirmed the people's commitment to worship and covenant faithfulness.

The Observance of Passover

The returnees also reinstituted the celebration of Passover, which symbolized their deliverance from captivity and God's faithfulness. Ezra 6:19-22 records this observance: "On the fourteenth day of the first month, the exiles celebrated the Passover. The priests and Levites had purified themselves and were all ceremonially clean. The Levites slaughtered the Passover lamb for all the exiles, for their relatives the priests and for themselves. So the Israelites who had returned from the exile ate it, together with all who had separated themselves from the unclean practices of their Gentile neighbors in order to seek the LORD, the God of Israel."

The Return under Ezra

Ezra, a scribe and priest, led a second group of exiles back to Jerusalem. His leadership focused on spiritual reform and the proper observance of the Law of Moses.

Ezra's Journey and Mission

Ezra's return was sanctioned by King Artaxerxes, who provided resources and authority for his mission. Ezra 7:6-10 highlights his journey and purpose: "This Ezra came up from Babylon. He was a teacher well versed in the Law of Moses, which the LORD, the God of Israel, had given. The king had granted him everything he asked, for the hand of the LORD his God was on him. Some of the Israelites, including priests, Levites, musicians, gatekeepers and temple servants, also came up to Jerusalem in the seventh year of King Artaxerxes."

Spiritual and Social Reforms

Upon his arrival, Ezra discovered that many of the returnees had intermarried with foreign women, contrary to the Law of Moses. This issue threatened the purity and identity of the covenant community. Ezra responded with a call to repentance and a covenant renewal, leading the people in a public confession and commitment to separate from these foreign influences (Ezra 9-10).

The Rebuilding of Jerusalem's Walls under Nehemiah

Nehemiah, a cupbearer to King Artaxerxes, led the third significant return to Jerusalem. His primary focus was on rebuilding the walls of Jerusalem, which were essential for the city's security and restoration as a political and spiritual center.

Nehemiah's Commission

Nehemiah received permission and support from King Artaxerxes to return to Jerusalem and oversee the rebuilding of the walls. Nehemiah 2:5-8 records his request and the king's favorable response: "I answered the king, 'If it pleases the king and if your servant has found favor in his sight, let him send me to the city in Judah where my ancestors are buried so that I can rebuild it.' Then the king, with the queen sitting beside him, asked me, 'How long will your journey take, and when will you get back?' It pleased the king to send me; so I set a time. I also said to him, 'If it pleases the king, may I have letters to the governors of Trans-Euphrates, so that they will provide me safe-conduct until I arrive in Judah? And may I have a letter to Asaph, keeper of the royal park, so he will give me timber to make beams for the gates of the citadel by the temple and for the city wall and for the residence I will occupy?' And because the gracious hand of my God was on me, the king granted my requests."

The Rebuilding Effort

Upon arriving in Jerusalem, Nehemiah inspected the walls and mobilized the people for the rebuilding effort. Despite facing opposition from neighboring leaders, such as Sanballat and Tobiah, Nehemiah inspired the people to work diligently and remain vigilant. The walls were completed in an astonishing 52 days, symbolizing God's favor and the resilience of the returnees (Nehemiah 4-6).

Spiritual Renewal and Covenant Commitment

The rebuilding of the walls set the stage for a significant spiritual renewal and covenant commitment, led by Ezra and Nehemiah.

The Reading of the Law

Ezra and Nehemiah gathered the people for a public reading of the Law of Moses. This event, held at the Water Gate, was marked by a deep sense of reverence and a renewed commitment to follow God's commands. Nehemiah 8:5-6 describes the scene: "Ezra opened the book. All the people could see him because he was standing above them; and as he opened it, the people all stood up. Ezra praised the LORD, the great God; and all the people lifted their hands and responded, 'Amen! Amen!' Then they bowed down and worshiped the LORD with their faces to the ground."

The Feast of Tabernacles

The people also reinstituted the celebration of the Feast of Tabernacles, which had not been observed in such a manner since the days of Joshua. This festival, commemorating God's provision during the wilderness journey, symbolized a renewed dedication to living according to God's instructions (Nehemiah 8:13-18).

The Covenant Renewal

Following the reading of the Law, the leaders and people of Israel made a solemn covenant commitment to obey God's commands. This covenant included pledges to avoid intermarriage with foreign peoples, observe the Sabbath, and support the temple and its services. Nehemiah 9-10 records the prayer of confession and the covenant document signed by the leaders.

Theological Reflections on Return and Restoration

The return from exile and the restoration period are rich with theological themes, including God's faithfulness, the importance of covenant renewal, and the hope of future promises.

God's Faithfulness and Sovereignty

The return from exile underscores God's faithfulness to His promises and His sovereignty over history. The prophecies of Jeremiah and Isaiah concerning the return were fulfilled, demonstrating God's control over the nations and His unwavering commitment to His covenant people.

Covenant Renewal and Community Identity

The restoration period emphasized the need for covenant renewal and the reestablishment of community identity. The returnees' efforts to rebuild the temple, walls, and spiritual life were central to their identity as God's chosen people. This period highlights the importance of maintaining a distinct and faithful community in the midst of a diverse and often hostile world.

Hope and Future Promises

The return and restoration also carried a forward-looking hope for the ultimate fulfillment of God's promises. The prophecies of Haggai, Zechariah, and others pointed to a future Messianic kingdom where God would dwell among His people in a restored and glorious Jerusalem. These promises provided hope and motivation for the returnees as they faced ongoing challenges.

Lessons for Contemporary Faith Communities

The return and restoration period offers valuable lessons for contemporary faith communities, particularly in areas such as resilience, covenant commitment, and hope.

Resilience in the Face of Opposition

The returnees' perseverance in rebuilding the temple and walls despite opposition serves as an example of resilience and faith. Contemporary faith communities can draw inspiration from their determination to uphold their commitments and trust in God's provision and protection.

The Importance of Covenant Commitment

The emphasis on covenant renewal and obedience to God's commands during the restoration period underscores the importance of maintaining a faithful and distinct community. Contemporary believers are encouraged to prioritize their relationship with God and uphold the principles of their faith in all aspects of life.

Hope and Vision for the Future

The prophetic promises of restoration and a future Messianic kingdom provided hope and vision for the returnees. Similarly, contemporary faith communities are called to hold onto the hope of God's ultimate restoration and the fulfillment of His promises, even in the midst of challenges and uncertainties.

Conclusion

The return from exile and the subsequent restoration of the nation represent a significant and hopeful chapter in the history of Israel. The events leading to the return, the challenges and achievements of the restoration period, and the enduring hope and future promises for the tribes of Israel are rich with theological and historical significance.

The return from exile underscores God's faithfulness and sovereignty, the importance of covenant renewal, and the forward-looking hope of ultimate restoration. The efforts of leaders like Zerubbabel, Ezra, and Nehemiah, along with the encouragement of prophets like Haggai and Zechariah, played crucial roles in guiding the returnees through this transformative period.

As we reflect on the return and restoration, we are reminded of the importance of resilience, covenant commitment, and hope in contemporary faith communities. The lessons from this period continue to offer valuable insights and inspiration for living faithfully and with vision in a complex and ever-changing world.

Bible Verse: Ezra 1:3 - "Any of his people among you may go up to Jerusalem in Judah and build the temple of the LORD, the God of Israel, the God who is in Jerusalem, and may their God be with them." This verse encapsulates the hopeful invitation and divine mandate for the returnees to rebuild and restore their nation, highlighting the central role of worship and community in their identity and mission.

Don't miss out!

Visit the website below and you can sign up to receive emails whenever Gregory Allen Parker publishes a new book. There's no charge and no obligation.

https://books2read.com/r/B-A-SLYZB-AGRHE

BOOKS 2 READ

Connecting independent readers to independent writers.

Did you love *The Twelve Tribes*? Then you should read *The Miracles of Elisha*[1] by Gregory Allen Parker!

[2]

Discover the awe-inspiring acts of Elisha, the prophet, through detailed narratives of his miraculous deeds and divine interventions. From his calling and faithful journey with Elijah to the healing of Naaman and the miraculous deliverance of Samaria, each chapter unveils a powerful story of faith, divine provision, and God's care for His people. With key Bible verses accompanying each miracle, "The Miracles of Elisha" brings the biblical accounts to life, offering profound insights and inspiration for readers today. Explore the miracles, reflect on their significance, and be encouraged by Elisha's unwavering faith in God.

---

1. https://books2read.com/u/4jZEPk

2. https://books2read.com/u/4jZEPk

About the Author

Pastor Gregory Allen Parker, a graduate of Trinity Theological Seminary, is a devoted pastor and acclaimed author of Christian fiction. With over two decades of ministry experience, his books explore faith's challenges and triumphs, offering readers inspiring and spiritually rich narratives. Celebrated for his compassionate pastoral care and insightful sermons, Pastor Parker's storytelling reflects his deep understanding of Christian values. When not writing or preaching, he enjoys family time, community volunteering, and the outdoors, continuing to inspire and uplift through his faith and craft.

www.ingramcontent.com/pod-product-compliance
Lightning Source LLC
Chambersburg PA
CBHW051838130726
47987CB00002B/600